## The door opened and a shape appeared

A tall looming shape outlined in the strange white light of the snow. The outline of a man.

Juliet screamed and went on screaming as he came nearer and nearer. She fell with him, their bodies hitting the carpet together and rolling over.

"Who are you?" she whispered, but she knew. He reached out a hand to turn on the light and she broke out hoarsely, "No, don't put on the light!"

"Are you afraid of facing me, Juliet?" he asked in icy mockery and she angrily snapped back.

"No!"

He laughed softly. "You've changed, you know. When you were seventeen you were downright skinny, flat as a boy front and back...." He paused, his voice mocking, "Nobody could say that now."

**CHARLOTTE LAMB** began to write "because it was one job I could do without having to leave the children." Now writing is her profession. She has had more than eighty Harlequin novels published since 1978. "I love to write," she explains, "and it comes very easily to me." She and her family live in a beautiful old home on the Isle of Man, between England and Ireland. Charlotte spends eight hours a day writing—and enjoys every minute of it.

In October, watch for *Besieged,* Harlequin Presents #1498, the first title in Charlotte Lamb's exciting new Barbary Wharf series. Written by one of the world's best-loved romance authors, Barbary Wharf is a six-book series set in the glamorous world of international journalism.

## Books by Charlotte Lamb

Don't miss any of our special offers. Write to us at the following address for information on our newest releases.

Harlequin Reader Service
P.O. Box 1397, Buffalo, NY 14240
Canadian address: P.O. Box 603,
Fort Erie, Ont. L2A 5X3

# CHARLOTTE LAMB

## shotgun wedding

*Harlequin Books*

TORONTO • NEW YORK • LONDON
AMSTERDAM • PARIS • SYDNEY • HAMBURG
STOCKHOLM • ATHENS • TOKYO • MILAN
MADRID • WARSAW • BUDAPEST • AUCKLAND

Harlequin Presents first edition August 1992
ISBN 0-373-11480-X

Original hardcover edition published in 1991
by Mills & Boon Limited

SHOTGUN WEDDING

# CHAPTER ONE

JULIET NEWCOME was just leaving her Chelsea flat when the telephone rang, and she almost did not go back to answer it because she had such a busy day ahead of her, but she had never found it easy to ignore the shrill insistence of a ringing phone, so she sighed and went back.

'Julie? It's me,' said her mother in a husky rush. 'I'm glad I caught you, I thought you might already be on your way to work, and I have to leave at once if I'm to get the London train, and then it will take ages to get to Heathrow from the railway station ... oh, I do hate travelling.'

Frowning, Juliet said, 'Slow down, Mum—what are you talking about? Where are you going?'

'Well, that's just it. I only heard myself this morning ... well, last night, well, in the middle of the night.' Shirley Mendelli's incoherence did not surprise her daughter, who was quite accustomed to it. It was one of the traits Juliet was glad she had not inherited. She knew she looked very like her mother; they were both tall, slim, with thick chestnut hair and blue eyes, and they both had good skins and oval faces, but in temperament they were very different. Juliet was calm and capable; Shirley was impulsive, impractical and volatile.

'Heard what?' Juliet patiently asked, but she should have remembered that you couldn't halt her mother's flow. Shirley would only tell the story her way—you threw her if you interrupted.

'I'm trying to tell you! Do listen, Juliet!' Shirley plaintively said. 'They rang at three o'clock this morning, which seemed like the dead of night to me, I was half asleep when I picked up the phone. Well, I couldn't book a plane then, of course, everything was closed for the night. I went back to bed but I couldn't sleep, so I got up again and packed my case and made sure the cottage was tidy, and I booked the first available flight to Italy...'

'Italy?' Juliet guessed then, her face sobering. 'It's Giorgio? He's been taken ill?'

Her stepfather had been in Italy for several weeks on a buying expedition, a task he undertook twice a year for the chain of shops they jointly owned. They sold luxury, handmade shoes, bought from various countries, but Italy was one of their main suppliers. Juliet had spoken to him only yesterday morning, when he had been in the best of spirits, so she knew that whatever had gone wrong must have happened suddenly.

'Arrested!' Shirley said dramatically, and Juliet gave a little gasp of shock and incredulity.

'Arrested? Giorgio? But whatever for?' Giorgio was the last man she would ever have expected to break the law. He simply wasn't the type; he loved the good life too much. *La Dolce Vita* was what he lived for, in fact: nice clothes, a comfortable home, a good car, a wife who adored him and fussed over him, elegant food, a little wine, a cigar after dinner. Giorgio had always seemed to Juliet to be one of the happiest men around. Over sixty, he was still a very handsome man, with silvery hair and dark eyes, a wonderful tan and a charming, endearing manner. She knew her mother thought the sun shone out of him, and he seemed to love her mother very much, too.

'Oh, I don't know, Julie,' her mother wailed. 'I couldn't make it out. I spoke to a policeman first, who said something about a driving offence. He had a thick accent, and in the shock of hearing the news my Italian deserted me—I didn't understand half what he said. Then they let me speak to Giorgio, but only for a little while and all he would say was that he was innocent, he didn't do it. He was almost in tears. He's gone to pieces—you know what he's like.'

'Do I not?' Juliet was smiling ruefully because Giorgio was one of those men who always needed a woman to look after them. His mother had been a fierce, dominating Sicilian who had given birth to twelve children, most of them girls, loved them possessively and ruled them with a rod of iron, which was why Giorgio had managed to reach the age of forty-five without ever marrying. His mother would not hear of it. Her other son, the eldest, had married a girl she had picked out for him, but Giorgio, her youngest child, was her favourite, and she would not let go of him. Giorgio had been too affectionate to fight her. He couldn't bring himself to hurt her feelings.

When her death had finally freed him, though, he had married the first woman he had met soon afterwards. The really surprising thing has been that he had married a foreigner, a visiting English tourist. It might so easily have been a disaster, that astonishing, unexpected marriage, but it hadn't, it had instead been a blazing success, and they were still happy over fifteen years later.

'So you see why I must get to him as soon as I can!' said her mother.

'Of course—poor Giorgio! He must be in quite a state. Would you like me to come, too? I'll have to rearrange a few appointments for today, but that won't be hard. I could book a late afternoon flight, I'm sure there must be one...'

'No, no, dear, I can manage on my own. I'd rather you stayed here, then if I need anything— money, legal help—I can ring you. We can't all three of us be away or who knows what might happen to the business?'

Juliet smiled wryly. 'Oh, I think it would stagger on for a few days, but I'll do whatever you want me to, you know that. Anything I can do now?'

'Just one thing—will you go down to the cottage at the weekend and make sure everything is OK? The workmen should have finished work on the new kitchen extension and be out of there—I meant to drive down to make sure they had done the job properly. Mrs Cottman, who comes in to clean the place for me, you know? Well, she was going to keep an eye on them, but her daughter has had a baby and she's gone to Leeds to look after them both, so I don't know what sort of state the cottage is in, and it's on my mind, so if you could...'

'Sure! It's Thursday, isn't it?' Juliet stared at the wall, mentally checking off her weekend plans. 'I don't have anything important on this weekend.'

Just a date with the man she was currently seeing, but that would have to be shelved. It was more important to set her mother's mind at rest. 'Look, I'll drive down tomorrow night. Just remember, if you need to speak to me after five tomorrow I'll be driving down to the cottage, so wait and ring me there after nine.'

'Oh, dear, it is a long drive, darling. Are you sure you don't mind?'

'Quite sure! In fact, I'll enjoy a break from London for a couple of days,' Juliet soothed. 'Don't worry about it. Just concentrate on Giorgio, give him my love, and make sure you get him the best possible lawyers. As soon as you arrive, get in touch with the Lazaro brothers—they've known him for years, and they're such good friends; I'm sure they'll be happy to help. And Mum . . . keep in touch, won't you?'

'Of course, darling. I must hurry or I'll miss my flight . . . bye, talk to you soon.' Shirley Mendelli flung the phone down and Juliet smiled wryly as she replaced her own. Really, she should be going with her mother. Mum was bound to get flustered and into a panic, and although she now spoke pretty fluent colloquial Italian, after her years with Giorgio, it would probably desert her faced with a worrying situation. Juliet hesitated, then decided to wait and see how her mother sounded next time she rang up. If Mum got out of her depth no doubt she'd ring tonight and she could always catch the next flight to Milan and join her.

She had a busy day ahead of her, visiting three of the London stores in turn, so she pushed all thought of her mother and Giorgio to the back of her mind for the moment, and hurried out to the garages adjoining the block of flats in which she lived, to pick up her small red estate car. It was a useful vehicle; she could carry quite a large amount of stock in the back of it if necessary, but it didn't take up too much room if you had to park somewhere in busy London streets.

It was typical of Juliet that she should be so practical in her choice of car, just as it was typical of her mother that she should have named her only daughter so romantically. Juliet disliked her own name: kids loved to make fun of classmates, and, everywhere she had gone at school, she had been greeted with falsetto shrieks of, 'Romeo, Romeo wherefore art thou Romeo?' or even, 'Who let you off the balcony, Juliet?' Fortunately, in time, most people had begun to call her Julie.

Except her father, she thought suddenly, grimacing. He had gone on calling her Juliet. Typical of him to be obstinate and unyielding in that, as in everything else. Jack Newcome's mind had set in concrete long before she was born; he had never changed while she knew him, and no doubt he never would. She had never been able to understand why her mother had ever married him.

Traffic was heavy that morning. It was nine o'clock by the time Julie reached her first call of the day: the Bond Street store. She parked in the alley at the back, but walked round to inspect the window display, standing on the pavement, her chestnut head to one side. Yes, it caught the attention, and, from the look of it, had cost very little, which was a big plus.

She was delighted with that spring's colours: daffodil-yellow, leaf-green, sky-blue. They lifted the heart as you looked at them, and the window-dresser here had produced an alluring effect with some clouds of pink gauze, a few sprays of artificial apple blossom, a brilliantly painted land-scape background. The delicate handmade shoes seemed to float above the clouds, among the blossom—you felt they must be as light as air and a joy to wear.

This new girl was talented; they must keep her. Julie made a mental note to tell the manageress to give the girl a small rise. It was a mistake to under-pay talented staff, Giorgio had told her when she began managing her first store. She bit her lower lip, thinking about her stepfather. What could have happened? He wasn't a careless driver; on the con-trary he was a very experienced one with a blameless record.

'Something wrong?'

The voice made her jump, swinging round, but she relaxed when she saw the young woman standing next to her. 'Oh, hello, Sandy. Sorry, I was miles away.'

'I thought you were hating the window display!'

'Good heavens, no! I love it,' said Juliet, and Sandy Carter gave a relieved grin, her brown eyes brightening again.

'Oh, good! I was pleased with it myself. Karen did it, the new girl. She's good, don't you think?'

'Very,' agreed Juliet, nodding. 'In fact, I was just deciding to give her a small rise. We must keep this girl, Sandy. She's the most promising window-dresser we've had for ages.'

'I'll do my best to keep her happy!' promised Sandy, and Juliet smiled at her.

'And your best is pretty good!'

Sandy had been managing the store for several years, and was very good at her job. Staff and customers liked her, yet she was very efficient; this branch had run like clockwork ever since she took over.

She grinned back at Juliet, pleased with her comment, and in a friendly mood they walked together through the front of the shop and into Sandy's little office. Juliet smiled and nodded to the two girls busy tidying the racks of shoes, but didn't linger to talk to them. 'I have a lot to get through today, Sandy,' she explained. 'I'm having to do my mother's job as well as my own, for the moment. She has had to go to Italy—something has happened to Giorgio...'

Sandy listened while Juliet told her all about Shirley Mendelli's phone call that morning, looking as startled as Juliet had felt, and expressed much the same disbelief. 'Giorgio, of all people! He can't have been drinking? Well, I know he likes the odd glass of *vino*, but he doesn't overdo it, does he?'

'Giorgio isn't given to extremes,' agreed Juliet. 'That's probably why he and my mother get on so well. It takes a man as easygoing as Giorgio to put up with her mood swings.'

'How did your own father...' began Sandy, then hesitated, because Juliet rarely mentioned her father. 'Sorry, that's not my business!'

Juliet made a wry face. 'Oh, it's no secret. My father never understood my mother, she drove him crazy. Their marriage was a disaster from day one, I imagine.'

She would never have told anyone else that, but Sandy was probably her closest friend; they had got to know each other while they were both working in the Oxford Street store, seven years ago. At that time, Juliet had been shy, self-conscious and unhappy, and would never have made friends with anyone if they hadn't done most of the work. Sandy was so different; cheerful, casual, friendly, she had been so easy to get on with that Juliet had got to know her almost without realising it.

A pocket Venus with brown eyes and gingery fair hair, Sandy was married to a travelling salesman who was often away for half the week, which Juliet knew she would hate, but which did not seem to bother Sandy.

She was always happy to see her husband, Tom, back again, but when he was away she didn't seem unhappy, maybe because she had an absorbing career of her own, and a great many friends. She and Tom lived in a modern block of flats, mostly occupied by young people, none of them with children. Sandy had rapidly got to know most of them, and her social life was a busy one, but she was a big success in her job and Juliet hoped they would keep her.

The trouble was, they were a small chain; just half a dozen shops so far, mostly around London, although they had opened one in Manchester recently. Shirley and Giorgio had moved up there for a few months, to see it launched and monitor its progress. If it was a success, they would open another next year, but they couldn't pay as much money as a bigger chain might be able to offer Sandy. If they continued to expand, one day, no doubt, there would be room for Sandy to move up into an executive position, which was what she wanted, Juliet was aware, but that was all very much a future dream, and not likely to happen for some years since they could not risk expansion until it became easier to borrow money at manageable interest rates.

'You never see your father, do you?' Sandy asked, breaking into Juliet's abstracted thoughts, and with a start of surprise Juliet shook her head.

'No,' she said in a flat, harsh voice, then hurriedly picked up the accounting sheets for the previous month, which were lying on the desk in an open folder. 'Well, we must get on, Sandy!' she said, her eyes on the neat rows of figures. 'Sorry, but not only have I got my mother's work to do; she wants me to go down to Cornwall this weekend. She's had some building work done, but hasn't had a chance to inspect it, so I promised to pop down there tomorrow.'

'Pop down?' repeated Sandy, half aghast, half amused. 'It will take you hours! And it's bound to be freezing down there.' She made Cornwall sound like the Arctic and Juliet laughed.

'I can't say I'm looking forward to that long drive, especially on a Friday evening, after a full week's work, but I don't want her fretting over the cottage while she's so upset over Giorgio.'

'But weren't you going to some posh ball with Adam?'

Juliet pulled a face. 'Yes, and I'm not looking forward to telling him I can't go.'

'Can't you drive down to Cornwall today, and get back in time for the ball?'

'No, I have several very important appointments; I can't put them off, and, anyway, I want to be near Heathrow just in case my mother rings up and says she needs me urgently in Milan. By tomorrow night she should have found out exactly what's wrong.'

Sandy nodded sympathetically. 'Yes, of course. Oh, well, Adam will understand; family has to come first.'

Juliet gave her a wry smile. 'Let's hope so. But it's his firm's annual party, all his bosses will be there, and Adam wants to make a big impression. He even came with me to buy my dress, to make sure I looked suitably ritzy, so he isn't going to be too pleased when he hears I'm going down to Cornwall instead, but I don't see how I can get back by Saturday night. I shall be exhausted after the drive down there. I doubt if I shall be able to face driving back almost at once.'

'No, I should say not,' agreed Sandy, but when Juliet talked to Adam York that evening he was by no means as understanding. In fact, he was furious.

He went red and stiffened, his blue eyes flashing sparks at her.

'You can't be serious! You must come! I can't go to the ball alone, people will think you stood me up! I'll look a complete fool!' Nothing could horrify Adam more than the prospect of looking a fool. Juliet knew that and looked at him ruefully. She realised why his dignity meant a great deal to him. He was a man from a poor background who was climbing the ladder of success so fast that it occasionally gave him vertigo, made his head swim and made him afraid of falling. He felt the need to appear completely in control, completely at his ease. He used dignity as an armour. It was his inner uncertainties that had attracted her, in fact, not that Adam would be too pleased if she told him so. He could be rather sweet and helpless, when he stopped pretending to be a big, tough executive.

'I'm sorry, Adam. I know how much it means to you, but it's a matter of priorities...'

His face tightened angrily. 'I see. And I come second to your mother's cottage, do I?'

'I didn't mean that.'

'Oh, yes, you did. Your mother asks you to drive hundreds of miles to check on her cottage, so you dump me and our date without a second thought. My career doesn't matter a damn to you, does it? I've explained over and over again how important this occasion is...the Chairman will be there! He always dances with a couple of the prettiest women—he might have picked you.'

'He might not even have noticed me!' Juliet muttered.

Adam snapped back, 'The wives and girlfriends of executives always get noticed! The higher you go in the company, the more important it is to have a presentable woman.'

'Oh, thanks. So that's what I am, is it? A presentable woman?' Juliet was seething, too, now, and had flushed bright pink. 'I'm not a possession of yours, Adam. You can't trot me out to be assessed by your boss once a year. Do I get marks out of ten? How do they work it out? A mark for clothes sense? A mark for good legs? What else do they judge a woman on? You'll be asking me to cook dinner for the whole board of directors, soon, to prove to them I can cook, too.'

'Oh, don't be so ridiculous!' he snarled, his hands screwing into fists as if he wanted to hit her, although Adam was far too polite to do anything of the kind. 'You know what I meant. It's vital for you to be with me this one evening of the year. It isn't too much to ask, is it? Everyone will be there— the managing director, my head of department, everyone! I've talked about you, they're expecting you . . .'

Their eyes met and she read his expression, frowning. Adam had boasted about her, she realised suddenly. Her family firm had been getting big publicity lately, with their expansion out of London. She was a very useful girlfriend for an ambitious man like Adam; if she didn't show up his pride and his ego would be dented. It wasn't that he would miss her; it was merely that he wanted to show her off. She hesitated, not knowing what to say, both irritated and sorry for him.

'Isn't there anyone else you could take?' she suggested at last, and he looked at her as if she was mad.

'Another woman? You really want me to take another woman?'

She fell silent, realising suddenly what she had said, and all that underlay the words. Adam sounded outraged, as if she had suggested some heinous infidelity, had told him to betray her. There was a fraught silence while they both stared at each other, and Juliet tried to say something, anything, to cover the discovery she had just made, they had both made.

Adam had been having a light supper with her, just a warm quiche with salad followed by fruit. He got up from the table, pushing back his chair with a violence that made it fall over, and walked, stiff-legged like a stork, to the door. Juliet followed him and watched him collect his expensive camel-hair overcoat, put it on and turn towards her, drawing on his tan leather gloves.

'There's nothing to say, is there?' he said. 'Either you come to the ball with me, or you don't, and we're finished. Let me know by tomorrow evening which way you decide.' He opened the front door and paused, his flushed face struggling to be polite. 'Thank you for supper—it was delicious.'

As the door closed she felt a bubble of hysterical laughter in her throat. How typical of Adam to become formal and courteous after issuing her with an ultimatum. Then she stopped laughing. Why hadn't she realised until now that she wasn't serious about Adam? Her mouth indented wryly; but *hadn't* she known? Had she ever thought of herself as serious, committed to him? She had drifted into the relationship gradually, not intending to get seriously involved—it hadn't entered her head that Adam thought she was serious, or that Adam himself might be serious.

She curled up on the carpet in front of the electric log fire which glowed on her small hearth, trying to sort out her thoughts, Adam's feelings. What exactly did she mean by... serious? What was she saying? That he was in love with her? The idea made her frown, then laugh shortly. No. Not that. Adam was not in love; he felt nothing so overwhelming.

He had probably decided, though, no doubt after careful thought, because that was Adam's way of reaching any important decision, that she would make a suitable wife for a rising young executive; and perhaps that was the right way to consider marriage—as a partnership. What, after all, had love to do with it?

No sane person would marry for love—that was no basis for choosing someone to live with, to bring up children with, was it? Juliet didn't trust love. Love was messy and explosive, it made you vulnerable, betrayed you and it didn't last; worst of all, it left you feeling like hell. She had been in love once, and the wound still ached on certain days, like the scars of some old battle. She never intended to let love happen to her again, and, luckily, so far she had never been in the slightest danger of caring that much for anyone else.

She had felt quite safe with Adam, she liked him, but not too much. He was no threat to her emotions, and yet he was good company. They had a lot of friends in common, and everyone felt that they made a nice couple; their mutual friends approved, and, although she had ignored the fact until now, so did their families. She should have guessed, meeting the smiles, the knowing looks, the little hints, from his mother, her own.

Why on earth hadn't she realised the way the wind was blowing? How had she stayed blind for so long? She could kick herself. Had she preferred not to know? It was so convenient to have a representable male as an escort, someone her mother and Giorgio liked, someone who knew most of her friends and had a busy career of his own, so that he understood the demands her job made— and also, admittedly, she did like Adam.

She bit her lip, her frown deepening. Yes, she liked him—but not enough to think of spending her life with him, surely? Her blue eyes were troubled. It was just as well that this had happened. She had been warned, and now she had to make a very important decision. She was too tired tonight, though. She looked at her watch, and got up. She would sleep on it, decide tomorrow.

She must have been more tired than she realised, because she slept through her alarm and woke with a start to find that it was gone eight and she was going to be late for work.

It was a bad start to a difficult day; she was in a hurry from then on and had to shelve any thought of Adam and whether or not she wanted to end their relationship. It was only as she drove out of London, heading west along the motorway, that she admitted to herself that the decision had been made without her needing to think. She had not rung Adam, and silence was an answer in itself. He would know what it meant. If she had rung him, he might have tried to persuade her, or flown into another rage, and she was too tired to face either reaction. Adam would have no problem finding someone to take; he was not good-looking, but he was attractive—a tall, slim man with a thin face, smooth brown hair, and pale blue eyes. Sometimes she had had trouble conjuring up his face in her memory, it was true; Adam was not memorable. But he dressed well, he was very eligible and she knew other girls noticed him; he would soon find someone else.

I'll miss him, she thought, pulling a face. They had been seeing each other for months; he was a habit with her.

Oh, well. She sighed, making herself concentrate on the road. There was no point in regret for what could not be helped. Life wasn't easy, that was all. The motorway wasn't crowded, at least, that was something, and the news from Italy that afternoon had been comforting. Her mother's panic was over; Giorgio had been involved in an accident and had been accused of causing it but his lawyers had found witnesses who swore the other driver had been responsible for the crash. Giorgio and Shirley would be coming home in a few days, with any luck.

Some time later, after crossing the county line into Devon, she glanced at the dashboard clock; not too long now. She didn't enjoy driving long distances at night. It was March and the weather had taken a turn for the worse during the afternoon. The sky was cloudless, an icy wind blowing from the east. She was doing a steady seventy miles an hour and at this rate she should get to the cottage before nine. She decided not to stop for a meal. There was plenty of food in the store cupboard at the cottage; tinned or frozen. She would be happy with whatever she found.

Night had fallen, but there was a strange light in the sky—not the sulphurous glow of street lighting, something very different. Juliet screwed up her eyes in puzzled surprise, staring—what was it? It looked positively eerie.

Then she saw the first soft white flakes blowing across the windscreen and her heart sank. Oh, no! Not snow! She hadn't bargained for that when she had agreed to drive down here.

As she drove on westwards, the gentle drift of snow became a howling blizzard, and she began to think she wasn't going to make it, but the roads were not yet impassable. An hour later she finally reached the isolated little cottage at the edge of moorland, within earshot of the sea.

It had been built for a shepherd, nearly two hundred years ago; a simple little dwelling, two rooms downstairs, two up, flint walls, a slate roof. It had been modernised now, of course, and much extended. There was a bathroom, a cosy country kitchen, even central heating, and Juliet pulled up outside the front door with a long sigh of relief. Her gloved hands seemed to be frozen to the wheel, and she was cramped and shivering. She found the front door key, dived out, unlocked the cottage, then ran back to fetch her suitcase before gratefully slamming the front door behind her.

It only took a short while to make the place a warm and welcoming home; she put on lights, turned on the oil-fired central heating, made up her bed, switched on the electric underblanket in it, unpacked, opened a can of tomato soup, heated it, cut some of the new loaf of bread she had brought with her, toasted it, and sat down to eat her supper at the kitchen table.

Her first spoonful was on its way to her mouth when the phone rang, and she dropped soup all over herself with a cry of shock.

Jumping up, she dabbed herself with a tea-cloth while she was running to snatch up the phone. 'Hello?' she breathlessly said, expecting to hear her mother's voice.

There was a silence, then a husky male voice said, 'Mrs Mendelli?'

Disappointed, Juliet said flatly, 'No, I'm afraid she isn't here at the moment. She's in Italy, with her husband. Would you like to leave a message?'

There was another silence, then he said, 'Who is that?'

For no reason she could have explained, that voice made a shiver run down her back; an instinctive, atavistic shudder. She didn't recognise the voice, yet she almost didn't answer, which was crazy.

He had only asked who she was! A perfectly natural question, wasn't it? What is the matter with you? she asked herself.

'I'm her daughter,' she slowly said, and got a second shock when she heard the phone click, and realised he had hung up without another word. After a surprised pause, she replaced her own phone, frowning. How rude.

She went back to the table and sat down. Well, at least her soup was still hot. She finished her meal hungrily, but couldn't stop thinking about the phone call. Who could it have been? They had no near neighbours here; the nearest house was a mile off, nearer the sea, but if it had been someone she knew he would have said so—he wouldn't have hung up without a word.

She hadn't felt nervous about being here alone until then, but as she washed up and tidied the kitchen before going upstairs to bed she felt distinctly jumpy. Every little noise made her nerves prickle. She kept freezing, listening—was that the wind rustling the trees, or the sound of someone creeping around the house? Was that the crack of a twig underfoot outside, or the noise of the central heating in the pipes?

She was here to check up on the building work her mother had had done, so she went on a tour of inspection, telling herself it was not because she wanted to make sure there was nobody else in the house. She liked the new extension, which was to be a dining area leading out of the kitchen. The pine panelling and floor looked wonderful, and it had all been left very neat and tidy.

The doors and windows were all securely bolted, there was no sign of anyone outside, the snow glistening, pure and untrodden in the lights of the house, and so, wryly making a face at her own reflection in a mirror as she passed, she turned off the downstairs lights at last, and went up to bed just before ten. How could she have let herself get so jumpy over a phone call, and the rudeness of some total stranger?

She had a bath, her weary muscles relaxing in the warm, scented water, and then she put on the warm, blue-striped pyjamas she had brought with her, knowing how cold it could be in the cottage, even in March. Her bed had warmed up nicely, though, so she switched off the electric blanket and the bedside lamp and snuggled down with a sigh. She was exhausted; she fell asleep within minutes.

She woke with a jolt some time later, and sat up, eyes wide yet blank with sleep, trembling as if from a nightmare. She didn't know where she was for a second and stared around, slowly recognising the shadows of the furniture, remembering why she was here.

The room was filled with the eerie light she had seen on her drive; the reflection of the moon and stars on the snow outside, a magical, disturbing light which made her shiver.

She was about to lie down again when she heard the creak of a floorboard outside, on the landing. Her heart crashed into her ribs; she stared fixedly across the room—there was someone there, outside her room.

Before she had time to think the door began to open and she saw in the strange white light of the snow a shape appear in the doorway, a tall, looming shape. The outline of a man.

# CHAPTER TWO

JULIET wanted to scream, but she couldn't—her throat seemed numb, her mouth was open but no sound came out, although inside her head she was screaming, and the moment stretched like a tortured nerve, on and on, while she stared and the dark shape in the doorway did not move.

Then suddenly he did, taking a long, silent stride towards the bed, and that seemed to free her voice. She did not scream, but she gave a high, shaking cry, shrinking back against the headboard of the bed, her wide eyes watching him like the terrified eyes of a trapped animal watching the predator, unable to flee because of its own fear. He was wearing black from head to foot; a leather jacket which shone with wet snow, black trousers, black boots. His head was black, too; she saw the sheen of his jet-black hair. If she could only see his face she might not be so scared, but the pale snow light did not illumine his features—it merely shimmered across his face in an unearthly way.

He was only a few feet away by the time she had managed to start thinking. What was she doing, sitting there, waiting for him? She had to get away.

She scrambled off the bed and began to run towards the open door, but he moved faster, launching himself at her like a rugger player, his hands reaching for her. Juliet screamed then, and went on screaming as she fell, with him, their bodies hitting the carpet together and rolling over and over.

'Who's going to hear you?' he whispered hoarsely, and he was right, of course. Nobody would hear her, because there were no houses within earshot—this was a very isolated cottage, deliberately chosen because it stood a mile from any other habitation, a place out of the rush of modern life, a place to be safe and peaceful. There was irony in that thought now.

'My husband will be back from work soon, he'll be here any minute...' She tried to sound convincing, but he laughed.

'Oh, I'm really scared,' he whispered in that deep, husky voice, and she recognised it, she realised that it had been familiar from the start.

He was the man who had rung earlier. He must have been checking to see if anyone was in the cottage, and when he knew she was there alone...

Who was he? she thought desperately. She had this strange, disturbing feeling that she knew him. Her heart pounded against her ribs; she couldn't bear it, the thought of what he might plan to do to her. She suddenly rolled away, meaning to get up and run, but he was more quick-thinking than she was, his arm shot out and clamped her by the waist.

She lay on her side, facing away from him, trying to push his hand down, struggling violently, and he moved closer, forcing her into intimate body contact, his chest against her back, his thigh touching hers, his other arm sliding under her to hold her even tighter.

Juliet was breathing so rapidly that it hurt, and she was sobbing soundlessly, tears hot in her eyes. With another shock of fear she felt one of his hands move up. Her pyjama jacket had come undone in the struggle and he pushed it softly aside, slid a hand inside and touched her bare breasts with his fingertips, stroked her hard nipples, a light, caressing slide of flesh on flesh which made her jack-knife in recoil, trying to get away from him, while she moaned, 'No!'.

This time, though, he didn't try to stop her. He let her break free, let her struggle shakily to her feet, always expecting to be dragged back, like a mouse which a tormenting cat allows to escape only to snatch it back a second later.

He just sat up and watched her, as she ran for the door, trembling and uncertain, her mind in panic.

She had to get away from him; her head whirled with hurried plans and fears. If she could get a head start she could get to the car, but then she realised that her car keys were in her handbag, which was in the bedroom, and in this weather to try to run across the moors, or even along the road to the nearest village, would be suicide. The snow cut them off as effectively as if this cottage were an island in the middle of a frozen sea.

'There's nowhere to run to, Juliet,' he said behind her, reading her mind.

She froze in the doorway, her feelings chaotic. She had thought she was going crazy, that the strange, tormenting familiarity she had felt had all been imagination, but now she knew it hadn't been.

'You...you...' She looked back and he was on his feet, but he wasn't chasing after her. He simply stood there, a tall, black shadow in the snowlit room, staring at her, and she stared back, beginning to glimpse features beneath the cap of thick black hair.

A long, straight nose, a firm chin, wide, hard mouth, and his eyes...those eyes...grey, cold, disturbing... She took a long, appalled breath. It was him.

'You can't get away, not this time,' he said, and again the words echoed in her mind.

'This time?' she repeated aloud, beginning to shake again.

'Even if you could start the car, you wouldn't get far. The snow is already wall-high. I had to abandon my own car half a mile from here and walk the rest of the way, and I thought I might not make it. And the telephone lines are down locally. That wind has caused all sorts of damage, and the snow is causing more.' He sounded so matter of fact—how could he talk that way, seem so at ease, while her ears rang with memories she had tried to bury fathoms deep years ago?

'Who are you?' she whispered, but she knew, she had recognised him when he'd spoken her name. Perhaps she had even recognised his voice when he'd rung earlier. Something in the timbre of that voice had made the hair stand up on the back of her neck, sent dread spiralling through her. She hadn't quite put it all together—her subconscious hadn't told her conscious mind what it knew—but somewhere inside her head she had known, she realised that now.

'You know who I am,' he said with derision, reading her mind again, and that disturbed her even more. She did not want him reading her mind, guessing at her thoughts and feelings, all her reactions. She needed to put a mask upon her face and hide herself from him.

'I don't,' she lied, hoping it would be true and knowing that it wasn't.

He reached out a hand to the bedside lamp and she broke out hoarsely, 'No, don't put on the light!'

She didn't want to see his face, she didn't want to know for sure, because in this strange snowy light there was something dreamlike, mysterious, unreal about being here with him, and if he put on the light he would break the spell, bring them both out into the real world.

'Afraid of facing me, Juliet?' he asked in icy mockery.

She angrily snapped back, 'No!'

'You prefer it in the dark?' His voice held double meaning; she felt heat rise in her face.

'I'd prefer you to go away...now!'

He laughed softly. 'Don't you want to see how much I've changed? You've changed, you know. Even in the dark I could tell that. When you were seventeen you were downright skinny, flat as a boy, front and back...' He paused, and then went on, his voice mocking, 'Nobody could say that now. You have a very sexy body.'

'Shut up!' she broke out.

He talked on over her. 'Beautiful breasts...'

'Shut up!' Her face was burning now. His words conjured up the vision of his hand inside her pyjama jacket, the cool brush of his fingers on her bare flesh, and she was so angry she shook with it.

'Y-y-you had no right! T-touching me like that!' she stammered, her throat rough. 'You scared me senseless. I thought ... I didn't know, did I? That it was you. I thought it was someone who'd broken in ... any minute, I thought, I might be killed.'

'I didn't intend it to happen that way,' he began, and she gave a furious laugh.

'No?'

'No,' he said impatiently. 'Look, I had to see you, and there was no answer at your London flat, or at your mother's, so I rang here, and when you answered I decided to drive down here right away.'

'And break in and attack me!' she accused.

'I did not attack you!'

'What do you call it, then? You knocked me off my feet——'

'I had to stop you running away—you were in a stupid panic!'

'You knocked me to the ground, and then you...' She put her hands to her flushed cheeks, trying to shut out the memory. 'You...handled me!' she spat at him.

'I'm only human—you were too close for comfort; as soon as I touched you my curiosity got the better of me,' he said without any sign of contrition.

'You mean you enjoyed terrifying me!'

There was a little silence, then he laughed shortly. 'Yes, maybe I did. I was angry, and ... yes, maybe

I did, and I'm not apologising, Juliet, not after what you've done to me.'

She was the one to fall silent, then, biting her lip. For a moment, neither of them said anything, then he began talking again in that soft, mocking, conversational tone.

'Even your hair is different. You wore your hair in a long tail, right down to your waist, I remember. When you walked along it swung about behind you, like a squirrel's bushy tail. I was always tempted to pull it. You've cut it off, haven't you? I felt how short it was ... and it curls; it never did that. I hope you haven't changed the colour, too. I loved it; conker colour, a bright, shiny chestnut.'

Juliet couldn't bear any more. Shakily, she said, 'I don't know why you're here, or what you think you're doing, but I don't want you here—go away!'

She had hardly finished speaking when he said harshly, 'Did you know my father had died?'

The shock seemed to knock the breath out of her. It was at least a minute before she said, 'No...' The word was half denial, half grief, because she had loved his father, far more than she had ever loved her own.

'A month ago,' he said, sounding as if he didn't believe her. '*The Times* carried an obit. You didn't see it?'

'No. I rarely read newspapers, except trade Press. I don't have the time.' Her mother couldn't have seen the news, either, or she would certainly have said something. She, too, had been fond of the old man, and she knew how close he and Juliet had been. Taking a deep breath, Juliet quietly said, 'I'm very sorry to hear he's dead . . . you'll miss him.'

He laughed angrily. 'I could hardly miss him more than I have for the last eight years. He hasn't spoken to me since the night you left.'

She was stunned into silence, and, before she could say how sorry she was to hear that, he turned abruptly and switched on her bedside lamp. The sudden brilliance blinded her for a little while, then her eyes focused on him, seeing him properly for the first time. He looked even taller, a lean and hungry man, and dangerous with it, his face so familiar that she wondered how she had not known it even in the dark, those chiselled features and cold eyes, that wide, passionate mouth.

He was assessing her, too, from head to foot, with raking insolence; and she hurriedly buttoned up her pyjama jacket under that stare, making his mouth flick upwards at one corner in silent derision.

That smile made her angry again, and she burst out, 'Don't try to make me feel guilty about your father. Have you forgotten what you did to me that night? How could I stay there after that?'

His face was hard. 'You had led me to believe that that was what you wanted, remember?'

Her flush deepened. 'I was seventeen! I didn't know what I was doing!'

His grey eyes lashed her. 'Oh, I think you did. You wanted to marry into my family, you wanted to be the next mistress of Chantries. You'd had your sights set on me for months—you followed me everywhere I went; every time I turned round, there you were, as clinging as a limpet. My God, you chased me relentlessly.'

She wanted to burst into tears, and at the same time she was angry enough to kill him, because it was true and yet it was all lies. She had followed him around everywhere, she had clung like a limpet, but not because she wanted to be mistress of his family estate. That hadn't entered into it. She wasn't the ambitious type. She wasn't a social climber, or a fortune hunter. She had been half child, half woman, head over heels in love and unable to hide it. All she had wanted was to be close to him, to be able to see him, watch him, listen to his voice. She had been infatuated, obsessed, almost possessed, and she hadn't thought about any future with him, or realised where her wild pursuit of him might lead.

'I didn't want Chantries!' she muttered, glaring at him. 'That part isn't true. I won't have you accusing me of that! You were the one who misunderstood... I was just a silly teenager who was having her first crush—it wasn't real.'

His eyes flashed, electric, deadly. 'Not real? A first crush?' She heard hatred in his voice. 'And for that you ruined my entire life?'

She paled, drawing a painful breath. 'I didn't——'

Harshly, he broke in on her, 'My father's last will only turned up a few days ago. He had locked it in a drawer in the library, nobody knew it was there. His lawyers didn't have a copy of it—they believed the last will was one which left everything to me, but then last week the executors were going through his papers, and they found a later one.' He paused, staring bitterly at her. 'He didn't leave Chantries to me.'

Juliet went quite white, her eyes horrified. 'He didn't? But...then, who inherits?' Simeon had been an only child, but she knew that his father had had a brother, who lived up north in Scotland, somewhere, and that he had had several sons. Had old Robert Gerard left his estate to one of his nephews? How cruel and unfair. It was so unlike him; she wouldn't have believed him capable of it. No wonder Simeon was so angry; he had every right to resent this.

He was staring at her fixedly, his skin dark with rage, his jawline clenched. Suddenly he said in an icy voice, 'The whole estate, money, land, everything, was left to our children.'

The shock was so intense that all the blood seemed to leave her body; she swayed, shivering, as if in a high wind, and for a moment almost fainted. He took two strides to get to her, caught her as she slumped, and put her on the bed, but she struggled against his hands, trembling, pushing him away, unnerved by his touch, and sat up on the edge of the bed looking dazedly at him.

'You didn't mean that.'

'Yes,' he bit out through tight lips.

'He couldn't have!'

'He did.'

'It can't be legal!'

'Perfectly legal, it seems,' he snapped. 'He knew what he was doing, he had made other wills, only this time he didn't inform his solicitor. But he followed the formula that had been used with his previous wills, and the wording was all perfectly correct. He left everything in trust for any children——'

She interrupted shakily. 'Oh! To *your* children, you mean.' Her mind scrambled ahead, guessing what he had come here to say. 'I see why you had to find me. You want to marry again, have children, and so you need a divorce.' She felt a stab of odd feeling as she said the word, maybe of pain because their strange, brief marriage had caused her such misery, and its ending would be as strange as its beginning. She forced a smile which wavered uncertainly. 'I wouldn't have thought you needed to get my agreement, not after all these years. It must be a straightforward procedure, surely?'

'No divorce!' he snarled, and she shrank from the look in his eyes. If anything, he had grown even angrier while he listened to her. 'You didn't let me finish. Just shut up and listen. The children must be ours, yours and mine.'

She gave a gasp. 'What?'

'You heard me. He was quite specific; only our issue counts. If we have divorced, or if we don't have children within two years of my father's death, the estate goes to my eldest cousin, Tony.'

'Simeon,' she whispered, appalled. 'Oh, I'm so sorry! How could he do it to you? It isn't like him to be so unkind.'

'You ran away,' he said fiercely. 'He blamed me for that. He never forgave me. I was his son, his only son, but I never mattered the way you did.

You were always his pet, he doted on you from the minute you were born.'

It was true, she couldn't deny it. There had been a very strong affection between her and Robert Gerard. He had been that sort of man—he had loved women and enjoyed their company far more than that of his own sex, although he had been a very masculine man, big and broad and energetic. A real countryman, always out on his land, working at something, and in his leisure time riding, fishing, shooting the rabbits and pigeons which raided his fields.

He had got on well with his farmworkers; he had been a kind-hearted man, generous and impulsive, in spite of a notoriously hot temper. He had never sulked, though, she thought, half smiling at the memory. He had flared up, roared and raged, and then tried to make amends as best he could to his victim, and people who had known him had usually loved him. He had never forgotten, though, that his family had been farming that land since the time of the Normans, or that his house stood on the site of an ancient motte and bailey castle, battered down during the Wars of the Roses. The present house had been built in 1700, after a fire had destroyed the Tudor building, but Robert Gerard had taught Juliet to be aware of the other dwellings which had stood there, and whose remants still littered the grounds and he, himself, had taken enormous pride in his family history.

It had been his wife who had first taken an interest in the small Juliet; indeed it had been Mrs Gerard who had suggested that name for her, although it had been enthusiastically accepted by her mother. Mrs Gerard had longed to have another child, a daughter, but after the birth of her first child, Simeon, she had developed complications and had had to have an emergency operation which had made it impossible for her to have any more babies. Juliet's father had been gamekeeper on the Chantries estate and his wife had worked part-time for Mrs Gerard in the house, taking the baby with her after the birth.

Simeon had been nine when Juliet was born, and had just gone away to boarding school. His mother had been lonely—having another child around the house had made it easier for her to bear her son's absence. She had been a tiny, delicate woman with a very sweet face, and already suffering from the wasting disease which had killed her some ten years later. Simeon had been at university by then, and Robert Gerard had been left quite alone in the beautiful old house set among tall oaks looking down over a slow-winding river. That had been when his deep affection for Juliet really began; he had clung to her, at first, because his wife had loved her, and then for her own sake.

'I loved him, too,' she told Simeon now, her blue eyes wide and defiant. 'He was more a father to me than my own ever was! Your father was a wonderful man, warm and generous and thoughtful. A pity you aren't more like him!'

'Oh, yes! It was very thoughtful and generous of him to leave me out of his will!' he said with vitriolic sarcasm, and she had to see his point.

'Yes, he shouldn't have done that,' she agreed huskily, looking down yet watching him through her lashes with confused uncertainty. She had many reasons for hating Simeon Gerard—she hadn't imagined that she would ever feel any sort of sympathy for him again—but obviously it must have been a terrible shock to him to discover that his father had changed his will. There had never been an instant's doubt that Chantries was to pass to Simeon; why else had he gone from university, where he had taken a science degree, to agricultural college to complete a specialised course in farming and estate management? He had spent years training to run Chantries, and now his father had snatched it away from him. It was grossly unfair. She frowned, watching his hard, unsmiling face. 'But can't you challenge the will? Contest it?'

'On what grounds? That my father was out of his mind when he made it? Do you really think I'm going to do that? I told you, the will is perfectly legal.'

'Isn't there a loophole anywhere?'

'None. If we don't have children, the estate goes to my cousin.' He fixed glittering, steely eyes on her. 'And that would be a disaster because Tony would probably sell it. He isn't a farmer, nor does he want to be ... he likes living in London, having a good time, spending money, and as soon as he can liquidate the estate he will settle down to spend every last penny of it.'

She believed him; Tony had always been a spendthrift, wild and undisciplined, brought up by a rather silly mother to be spoilt and selfish. Robert

Gerard had known just what sort of man Tony was—why on earth had he left Chantries to him, instead of to Simeon?

'It doesn't make sense,' she said aloud, her eyes puzzled. 'Why did he do it? He always talked as if nothing would make him happier than to know that you would one day run Chantries.'

'My father changed after you left,' Simeon muttered, scowling over her head. 'He grew bitter, and he blamed me for everything that had happened. He was lonely, but he wouldn't have me in the house—I wasn't welcome at Chantries any more.'

Juliet was shaken. 'You left, too? But maybe that's why—— '

'I didn't leave. I was thrown out. I lived with the MacIntyres in Rose Cottage for some months, until I realised I would never be allowed back home, then I moved into one of the farm cottages which happened to fall vacant when old Ben Smith died.'

'Oh, did he? I'm sorry,' she instinctively said, her mind's eye at once conjuring up the old man with his brown, weather-beaten face and stooped shoulders walking across the fields, his black and white sheepdog loping at his heels. They were the figures of her childhood, these people: old Ben and Mr Gerard and all the others she had known as a little girl. She had tried to shut the door on them all, for years, but Simeon had pushed the door open again and was forcing her to remember everything.

'He was ninety,' Simeon said in a gentler, half regretful tone. He had known Ben all his life, had gone around the countryside with him, learning country ways. She suddenly recalled one night when they had both gone with Ben to lie in bushes in a copse and wait for a badger family to venture out to hunt. It had been a magical experience; she could almost smell the damp earth, the crushed grass on which they had lain.

Simeon's voice broke through her memories. 'Yes, he had a good innings, and he'd enjoyed his life, which is more than we can all say. Even after he retired, he was always busy; he poached, of course, although I turned a blind eye and pretended never to guess.' He grinned and under her eyes became younger, more carefree, the way he had been once. Simeon had been a reckless, exciting boy, a teasing, protective man, until... Juliet winced and stopped thinking.

'The trouble is,' Simeon said, 'the Bens of this world have no place in modern farming. We have machines to do everything he did.'

'More's the pity,' she muttered, and he sighed.

'Yes. He was quite a character.'

'When you left Chantries, did you have to stop working on the estate too?' she asked, and he shook his head.

'No, I still worked on the estate. In fact, I've been running the place for the last few years, because my father's health began to deteriorate and he more or less gave up the estate management to me.'

She gave him a bewildered look. 'So he did start speaking to you again?'

'No,' Simeon said curtly, bitterness in every line of his face. 'We communicated in writing. I sent him notes and letters, and long memos, and he replied in kind. It was absurd.'

She bit her lip. 'Doesn't it sound as if he was sick? Mentally, I mean. It's not like him—his illness may have made him confused, might have changed his personality. Couldn't you make that the basis for contesting the will?'

'I'm not having my father's name blackened in some courtroom!' Simeon snarled, and she took a nervous step away from him. He had always been a dominant character, even as a boy, but since she last saw him he had become a formidable, alarming man. She wouldn't want to cross him, or find herself opposing him.

'I didn't suggest——' she began to stammer.

'That was what you implied—that I should challenge the will on the grounds that my father didn't know what he was doing. And I won't have it. I'd rather see Tony let loose on Chantries than have my father's reputation blackened like that.' His rage was disturbing, yet she was touched by it because of what it meant: an affection for his father which he had rarely allowed to show but of which she had always been certain.

There was a brief pause, then Simeon went on quietly, 'In a sense, I think he was mentally ill, at the end. He never went out, never saw anybody— he brooded on the past all the time, I gathered from Dr Manners. He kept me in touch with my father's condition, and he was worried about his mental state—oh, he didn't think he was going crazy, but he knew Dad was in severe depression, and he kept trying to talk him into seeing me, but Dad wouldn't listen.' Simeon shot her a sideways look, his brows lowering. 'There were photos of you and my mother everywhere around him, but none of me, of course.'

Was he jealous of her? she wondered suddenly, her blue eyes wide with shock. Had he always been jealous of the affection between her and his parents? He had been sent away to school and she had somehow moved into his place in the family—was that how he saw it?

Simeon grimaced. 'He pretended I no longer existed. He wouldn't let Dr Manners talk about me. Even when he wrote instructions to me about the farm, he was impersonal, as though I was a stranger, just an employee. He never wrote "Dear Simeon". He just headed everything "To The Farm Manager".'

'Oh, Sim,' she said, instinctively putting a hand on his arm. 'I'm so sorry...'

He stiffened, looking down at the slender, pale fingers touching his black jacket, and she went pink and snatched her hand away, asking hurriedly, 'What was wrong with him physically?'

Simeon gave her an odd look, his black lashes flicking down against his brown, weathered skin. 'At first the doctors weren't too sure—one of them even came up with some crazy theory that he was trying to give himself the disease my mother died of. I think they believed it was psychosomatic, but it turned out to be some obscure disease of the liver. I suppose he would have died of it, but actually what killed him was a heart attack. It was very sudden.' He stopped short, brooding for a few seconds, then added, 'And I never said goodbye to him.'

'Maybe he never meant that will to stand, maybe he would have changed it,' she suggested, trying to think of some way of comforting him, and Simeon looked harshly at her.

'It hardly matters what he might have meant. The legal consequences are all that matter, and they are very clear cut, aren't they?'

'I'm very sorry, Simeon,' Juliet whispered unhappily, meeting his angry grey eyes. 'I know how much it will hurt you to lose Chantries.'

'I don't intend to lose it,' he said through his teeth, holding her gaze insistently. 'You are going to give me a child to inherit the estate.'

For a long, dazed moment she didn't understand—she stared at him blankly, trying to grasp what he meant, and then what he had said sunk in, and her mind reeled with appalled realisation. A flame of red swept up her face, and then she went white, trembling violently because the very idea made her sick; it terrified her, the thought of letting him touch her, ever again, impose his body on her, the way he had once before, on their wedding night.

'No!' she whispered, the one word carrying all her reaction—the shock, the dismay, the sick recoil.

Simeon couldn't have failed to hear it in her voice, read it in her stricken face, but he watched her impassively, a hardbitten man who had been toughened and hardened by years of bitter estrangement from his father. This was no longer the man she had known all her life, but then she was not the starry-eyed adolescent he had known.

She had become a woman literally overnight, and the years since then had changed her radically, too. They had both been through a sort of hell since they'd last met, and she ached with regret as she looked at him, because she knew that what had gone wrong between Simeon and his father had been her fault, although she had never meant to separate them.

Almost pleadingly she said, 'You weren't serious?' She couldn't believe he had meant it. Nobody could be that ruthless and cold-blooded, could they?

His lips hardened, then parted just enough to bite out the one word, 'Yes.'

'No,' she denied, panic beating up inside her.

'I'm not asking you to do this for nothing,' he said coolly. 'You'll get a generous allowance from the estate once there's a child and everything is settled. I can't see that I'm being unreasonable. The whole situation is your fault—it is up to you to solve it in the obvious way.'

'I can't believe this is happening,' she said wildly, 'I can't listen to any more.' She stumbled towards the door again, but Simeon caught her arm and his touch made her cry out. 'Don't! Don't touch me!'

He didn't let go, he just bent towards her and said softly, 'This time will be different—you're not a virgin teenager any more, after all. You're a woman, and no doubt there have been other men in your life since you ran away.'

She felt herself flushing again, and her lashes dropped to hide the expression in her blue eyes. 'That has nothing to do with it,' she said huskily.

'I couldn't sleep with you in cold blood, I just couldn't.'

There was an odd silence and she glanced through her lashes at him, slightly alarmed to find him smiling crookedly.

'In hot blood, then,' he said, and there was a tormenting gleam in his grey eyes now. He let his eyes wander down over the supple curve of her body, and to her shame she felt heat growing inside her, felt a pulse begin to throb in her throat. She might hate him, but he still did something to her.

'No,' she refused again, her voice high-pitched, feeling as if she might faint any minute. 'Please, leave me alone, can't you? I'm sorry, but what you're asking is impossible, I couldn't do it!'

Simeon considered her face, his brows together, then shrugged. 'Well, it's the middle of the night and we're both tired after that long drive from London, so we'll leave it for now, and talk about it in the morning.'

He let go of her and turned towards the door and Juliet watched him with desperate uncertainty.

'What do you mean—talk in the morning? You can't stay here, you know. I won't let you.'

'Throw me out, then,' he said with casual arrogance, because he knew she wasn't up to doing that. He went out of the room and she heard him walk into the big master bedroom. 'Very comfortable,' he called back to her. 'This will be fine.'

She stood there indecisively for a moment, wondering what to do, and then chose safety first. She locked her bedroom door as noisily as possible, so that he should hear her.

'Goodnight, Juliet,' was all the response she got, in an amused voice, and then the muted sounds of him moving around the room, visiting the bathroom, the soft creak of the bedsprings and then the click as he switched off the light.

Juliet lay in her bed staring at the dark ceiling for half an hour, her mind in utter confusion, before sleep finally overcame her, and then her dreams were chaotic.

# CHAPTER THREE

JULIET woke up with a start and didn't remember, for a moment, what had happened last night. She lay looking at the ceiling with a blank expression, noticing the play of icy light across it, hearing the wind outside howling across the moor, and wondering why she felt so tired and flat, almost depressed. Her head ached and she didn't want to get up. Was she getting a cold? Or was it the arrival of snow that had upset her?

Then she heard a faint sound in the cottage and it all came back to her in a blinding flash. She sat up with a gasp, staring at her bedroom door.

He was here. In the cottage, on the other side of that door, moving about, whistling softly. Simeon. Her pale lips framed the name silently. Simeon. Her husband.

She had pushed the memory of her brief marriage to the back of her mind so many years ago that she found the fact of it incredible now, just as she had found it the day she'd stood beside him in a register office, going through the civil ceremony which made them man and wife, looking sideways at him through her lashes in dazed disbelief. She might have tried consciously to suppress those memories, but she found that she had forgotten nothing. Everything about that day must have been burnt into her unconscious mind; she could summon up even the tiniest detail now.

She had been wearing her best dress, but it had hardly been suitable—a simple blue dress meant for a schoolgirl to wear at weekends, nothing special or very pretty. Her father didn't believe in spending good money on anything he felt was unnecessary, and pretty clothes for his only daughter came into the category of 'unnecessary'.

He had been there, to make certain it really happened; a grim, hostile presence in his only suit, a heavy country tweed he had had for years and wore at all formal occasions, even funerals, although for those he added a black armband around one sleeve of his jacket. She had almost expected him to have his shotgun over his arm, but Jack Newcome was too conventional for that. He had left it at home, although the threat of it smouldered in his sullen eyes every time he looked at her and Simeon.

He had found them together, after the harvest festival dance, lying in each other's arms, in the sweet-smelling, long grass under the heavy-laden apple trees in the orchard behind Chantries, and he had had his gun then. He had levelled it at Simeon, murder in his eyes, and Juliet had screamed, believing he meant to shoot.

'No, Father!'

He had looked at her, skating a disgusted look over her, silently commenting on her unbuttoned blouse, the glimpse that gave of her tiny, pale breasts, the way her skirt had ridden to her upper thigh, leaving her long legs bare. His face contemptuous, he had spat out an insult, called her something vile that had made her flinch, turning a shamed scarlet, and that had brought Simeon to his feet, his face dark with rage.

'Don't use language like that to her!'

'What else is she, then?' Jack Newcome had said, his mouth distasteful.

'Nothing happened, man!' Simeon had angrily protested, and her father had given a sneering laugh.

'Don't bother to lie to me. I know what I saw before you heard me coming.'

Simeon's flush had deepened. 'Look, Jack——' he had begun and the older man had snapped at him.

'Mr Newcome to you after tonight!' Then reproach had shown in his eyes. 'I never thought you'd do this to me, Mr Simeon. Not your father's son. As for her, well, I can't say I'm surprised. She's her mother's daughter, after all. I knew it would come out in her sooner or later, but I'd hoped to get her married off first. I won't be shamed in front of the whole county again, Mr Simeon. I had enough of scandal and gossip when my wife ran off with her fancy foreigner—I won't be made a laughing stock a second time.'

He had still had the gun pointed at Simeon, and his finger had been on the trigger, crooked as if to squeeze. Juliet had been so terrified that she had begun to scream again, and that had brought old Robert Gerard from the house, hurrying down the rough grass of the orchard path, his breathing noisy.

'What in heaven's name is all this noise? What's going on?' he had asked, staring in stunned surprise at the tableau he found under the trees; the heavy-set gamekeeper, the trembling, sobbing girl, and finally his own son.

Simeon and Jack Newcome had begun to talk at once, and Robert Gerard had broken in on them, impatiently. 'I can't listen to all of you. Jack, you tell me, and for God's sake lower that gun—is it loaded?' He had read the answer in the other man's grim face and gone on gruffly, 'What's the matter with you? You know better than to point a loaded gun at someone.'

The two older men had known each other all their lives. Her father had worked on the Chantries estate since leaving school; he was an excellent gamekeeper, he knew every aspect of his work, and he was temperamentally suited to it. He was up before dawn and out in the woods and fields, each day—and then after a few hours' sleep at night, he was always out again, on the alert for poachers after pheasants or partridge or even rabbits. The energetic lifestyle had seemed to suit him; he was a tough and physically wiry man, even though he was fifty; could walk miles without tiring.

Even the necessary solitude in the woods had seemed to suit him because he was quite happy alone; indeed was usually silent when he was in company, with one exception. Robert Gerard. The two men had seen each other most days and Jack Newcome was usually quite relaxed and easy with his employer, but not that night.

'I just caught them at it,' he had muttered, without lowering his gun. 'Did you know what was going on? I've had my suspicions lately, you must

have had yours—why didn't you tell him to leave
her alone?'

'What are you talking about?' Robert had asked
incredulously, and Juliet had closed her eyes, tears
rolling down her face.

Her father had bitterly given his side and Robert
Gerard had turned on his son with angry questions.
Simeon had shouted back at him, and then the three
men had all snarled and shouted at each other
across and around her while she'd just stood there,
shaking and terrified.

She had never heard her father speak like that
to Robert Gerard. Her father had always respected
his employer. She would have said Robert Gerard
was as close to being his friend as anyone in the
world.

That was why he had been content to allow Juliet
to spend so much time up at Chantries, especially
after her mother had gone.

Juliet had been eleven years old when her mother
had run off with Giorgio after a holiday she had
taken in Sicily with her aunt. Aunt Dora had always
dreamt of seeing Sicily but had been afraid of going
alone, her head full of tales of bandits and
kidnapping, so she had invited Shirley Newcome
to go with her. It had only been for a fortnight, the
first real holiday Shirley had had since her marriage. Jack Newcome didn't believe in holidays,
especially abroad, and he hadn't wanted his wife
to go, but for once she had had the courage to insist
on her own way, and that holiday had torn their
lives apart.

Her mother had met Giorgio and fallen madly in love, and hadn't come back. At the time, Juliet had felt betrayed, abandoned, but now with adult hindsight she could understand why her mother had chosen the man she loved rather than her child. When they talked about it, later, her mother had said frankly, 'After twelve cold, empty years buried in that place with your father, being with Giorgio was like coming alive again. I was so happy, darling. I couldn't bear to go back to Jack. I agonised over leaving you, and I know it must have hurt you, but I badly wanted you to be with us, and I kept hoping I would get you back once the divorce went through. I didn't believe he would be allowed to keep you. After all, he was never home, and he had never shown any interest in you. My lawyer was so confident that I would get custody of you. We didn't reckon on Mrs Gerard taking you over altogether.'

'I think Dad kept me simply to spite you,' Juliet had wryly said.

'I've no doubt about it! He was such a hard man!'

The court had decided to leave Juliet where she was, granting custody to Jack Newcome, but her mother had had the right to see her at least once a week, if she chose.

'Once Giorgio and I were living in London, I suggested that I should come down to Devon every other week, and you should visit us alternate weeks, but your father wouldn't co-operate. He wouldn't let you go out with us when we came to you. He made us sit in that cottage, with him there all the time, staring at us, like some horrible great basilisk, terrifying the life out of poor Giorgio.'

Juliet had giggled. 'Oh, I remember those visits!' They had been difficult and embarrassing for her, too.

Her mother had sighed. 'And as for you paying us any visits, he wouldn't hear of it. He said he couldn't spare the time to take you to London, and he would not let you travel alone. I felt so guilty, but we couldn't afford the time and money for weekly visits then, darling.' She had given Juliet a wistful, pleading look. 'Did you hate me?'

'No, of course not,' Juliet had said, knowing that that was what her mother wanted to hear, and after a while it had been true because her father had made her so afraid of him that she had gone over to her mother's side in their feud. 'I didn't blame you for wanting to get away fom Dad.' Her mother had written often, had always remembered her birthday, and Christmas. To be fair to him, her father had never suppressed those letters and cards, or held back the gifts her mother had sent her. It was true, too, that he had rarely said a word against her mother, but then he had never mentioned her at all, if he could help it.

It was as if he had expunged his ex-wife from his memory, beginning with the day he had had everything she'd left behind her cleared out of the cottage and burnt on a huge bonfire in the garden.

Juliet had watched from her bedroom window, pale and frightened by the destruction. She could still remember the smoke curling up, the grey sky through bare branches, the smell of autumn leaves, her father's grim face as he moved around the bonfire. Even at that age Juliet had felt the obstinate, unyielding nature behind his actions, and been disturbed by it.

The night he had found her in Simeon's arms he had looked just like that, a cold, grim man who never forgot or forgave, and all their denials and attempts to explain had made no impact on him.

Robert Gerard had been almost as angry, in a very different way. He had put an arm around Juliet, muttering roughly, 'That's enough, Jack. Can't you see, you're terrifying the child? Take her home now. We'll talk about this in the morning, when we've slept on it.'

'I'm not having her in my house again,' Jack Newcome had grated. 'I'm finished with her.'

Juliet had given a small, shuddering cry, and Robert Gerard had tightened his hold on her, putting his chin down against her tumbled hair.

'Jack, for heaven's sake!' he had protested, but her father had already turned to walk away, as if having said his final word.

Then Simeon had suddenly said, 'I'm going to marry her!' and both older men had stared at him in waiting silence.

Simeon had stared back at them, his face pale and grimly set. 'But she has to be married from her own home, not from ours, or there would be gossip, and that's what you want to avoid, isn't it?'

Her father had considered him for a long moment, then had given Robert Gerard a questioning look.

As pale as his son was, Robert had stared at the clear, autumn night sky, his brows together as he thought it over, then he had looked back at Jack Newcome and given him a sharp nod.

And so it was settled, and Juliet had gone home that night, with her father, in unforgiving silence, to wait for her wedding day, after which she was to move in to Chantries. Simeon and his father had decided that a honeymoon was essential, to give a more normal appearance to that hurried, hole-and-corner wedding, so the bride and groom had driven straight from the register office to a hotel in Taunton, to spend a few days, but the very next morning Juliet had got up early, without waking Simeon, and stolen out of the hotel and out of his life, leaving a brief note.

> It is all a mistake, I couldn't bear to go through last night ever again and I don't want to be married. Please divorce me, or have the marriage annulled or whatever you like, but don't come after me because I couldn't bear to see you again, not ever. I'll be OK—I'm going to my mother.

She had had just enough money for a coach to London, and had sat in a tense silence all the way, feeling like a fugitive, and afraid all the time of being caught and taken back. It had been an enormous relief to reach her destination. Shirley and Giorgio had welcomed her with open arms, if a good deal of surprise. They had not heard about the marriage, and she hadn't been able to bring herself to tell them anything of what had happened.

'Have you left school?' her mother had asked, and she had nodded.

'And I want a job,' she had said.

'You've got one!' Giorgio had cheerfully agreed. 'A job and a home—with us, Julietta.'

Tears had come into her eyes. 'Are you sure I won't be any trouble?'

'Trouble?' Giorgio's dark eyes had been liquid with emotion; he was a very affectionate, soft-hearted man. 'Oh, my dear girl, no. We have always wanted you—this is your home. It makes us both very happy to have you with us.'

'We've got plenty of room,' her mother had said with her more practical approach, but she had been beaming. 'Come and see, darling.'

She had taken Juliet to see her new bedroom, a pastel-painted room which was light years away from the austerity of her bedroom in the cottage where she had grown up. Alone, Shirley had asked her shrewdly, 'What's wrong, darling? We're delighted to have you, but what exactly pushed you into coming? A row with your father?'

She had longed to confide in her mother, but she had been afraid that her mother would be aghast and furious at what she heard. What if her mother thought she was to blame? She remembered the disgust in her father's face when he had confronted her and Simeon—she couldn't have born it if her mother looked at her like that.

So she had lied, and nodded. 'Y-yes, he...I...'

Her stammering had aroused her mother's protective instincts and Shirley had put her arms round her, hugging her.

'You poor kid! What did he do? He didn't hit you?'

'Oh, no!' Juliet had said. 'He's never hit me...' She had whitened, remembering her father's face. 'He just talks to me... looks at me as if I was...' She had broken off, biting her lip.

Her mother had made a face. 'I know just what you mean. Your father is old-fashioned. I suppose he didn't want you to grow up? I wondered how he would cope with a teenage daughter! Well, don't you worry, I'll look after you, he isn't bullying you with me around!'

'What if he comes after me?' Juliet had whispered.

'If he does, he'll have me to deal with! He's had you long enough—now it's my turn to look after you. I'd never have left you with him if I hadn't thought he loved you. I'd have fought to the death to keep you. Don't you worry, it will all be sorted out, and you needn't see him if you don't want to.'

'I never want to see any of them again,' Juliet had said.

She had begun to work in the shop which Shirley ran, while Giorgio was busy with a second store he had opened in Knightsbridge, not far from Harrods. For a few months Juliet had been haunted by everything that had happened, had kept expecting Simeon, or her father, or Robert Gerard, to turn up, but they had never come, and she had gradually pushed it all to the back of her mind. Her new life had occupied her every waking thought. She was young and living in London, one of the most magical cities in the world. She had refused to be unhappy.

Eight years had gone by without anything disturbing her busy days, but now, out of the blue, Simeon had turned up again.

She was dazed by the news he had brought. Robert Gerard's death was a grief to her, but even more of a shock was the news about his will. It had been unjust of him to leave Chantries away from Simeon, but even so Sim surely couldn't really have expected her to take his proposition seriously? Could he?

A sharp rap on the bedroom door made her jump, her nerves shredded.

'Up you get, Julie. The coffee's made and I'm just going to cook some breakfast,' his deep voice said, and she managed a husky reply.

'I'll be five minutes.'

He laughed shortly. 'I'll believe that when I see you.'

Challenged, she raced through her washing and dressing, and made it downstairs in about seven minutes, just in time to see Simeon put a dish of grilled bacon and mushrooms on the table.

He sat down then, raising a black brow at her. 'Amazing! You made it!'

She ignored that, accepting the cup of black coffee he had poured her. 'Where did you get the bacon and mushrooms?'

'I stocked up at a garage shop en route last night, in case you didn't have much fresh food,' he said, offering her the dish of food.

'Thank you, they smell delicious,' she said, feeling very hungry.

They ate in silence for several minutes, then, as they both took toast and spread it with marmalade, Simeon said, 'The snow is knee-deep this morning—did you notice?'

She hadn't and threw a startled glance at the window. All she could see of the garden was a white desert, crisp and untrodden except for a few tiny bird footprints scattered here and there. The snow was banked up to the top of the garden wall. That meant the roads must be blocked.

Nervously lowering her lashes, she watched Simeon. He was no longer looking quite as sinister as he had last night in his black leather jacket and black thigh boots. He had clearly shaved, and showered; his black hair was smoothly brushed and he was wearing jeans with a ribbed white sweater over a thin, powder-blue cotton shirt. He looked relaxed and casual, but Juliet didn't trust him any more than she would trust a basking shark. He looked across the table at her with an expression in his grey eyes that made her tense.

'We won't be able to leave, so we have plenty of time,' he said, and she unguardedly repeated the last word, her face bewildered.

'Time?'

'Time to . . . talk,' he murmured, lazily assessing her from head to toe in a deliberately tormenting fashion. 'And other things.'

Her colour rose again. The talking wasn't that alarming; it was the 'other things' that bothered her, but she didn't say so. She was going to have to watch what she said to him; he was in a mischievous and dangerous mood. He might be smiling and relaxed on the surface, but she knew that underneath that sunny façade the same anger and hostility simmered, and at any moment he might unleash them.

'Some more coffee?' he offered.

She absently took some, murmuring a stiff, 'Thank you.' She couldn't stay here with him—but how was she to get away?

'How is your mother?' he asked politely.

'Very well,' she told him, staring at the window with dismay. A flurry of snowflakes was whirling past. Simeon caught her look of consternation and followed her gaze. He smiled.

'Oh, dear, snowing again. We may be stranded here for days.'

'The snow ploughs will come out to clear the roads soon,' she thought aloud.

'The main roads,' he corrected. 'They won't clear this road yet—I'd imagine very few people use it in winter.'

She gave him a sharp look, frowning. 'How did you know about this place, anyway? How did you find it?'

He shrugged. 'I made a lot of phone calls late yesterday afternoon, after I got to London and discovered that you had left work and that you weren't at your flat. I rang your mother—no reply there, either—I rang all your shops and finally got on to someone who said you were in Cornwall.'

A suspicion crossed Juliet's mind. 'Was that the manageress of the Bond Street store, by any

chance?' He nodded and she thought aloud, 'Wait
until I see Sandy again! She knows that it's a
company rule never to give out any personal details
about a member of staff to a stranger!'

His eyes glinted with amusement. 'Maybe she
forgot.'

Juliet viewed him witout any answering spark of
humour. 'You didn't tell her...anything...did you?'

'That we were married, for instance?' he mocked,
watching the colour rise in her face.

The very idea of Sandy knowing her long-buried
secret made her want to scream, and he knew it.
He held her in suspense a moment longer, grinning
in a way that made her want to hit him, then shook
his head.

'No, I didn't need to. I just said I urgently needed
to talk to you about a death in the family, and for
some reason she seemed to think I was in Italy, so
she told me you were in Cornwall. She muttered
something about your mother, so I wasn't sure if
you were there with her or not, and she didn't know
the address or phone number, but getting both
didn't take me long.'

'I bet!' she said bitterly, and he looked even more
amused, as if she had flattered him, which certainly
had not been her intention.

'Well, Mendelli is hardly a common name in
England. I just went into a reference library and
looked up the telephone directories for Cornwall,
then rang this number to check you were actually
here. You answered, so I got in my car and set off.
I had a detailed map, so finding the nearest village
wasn't difficult, either, and I stopped at the garage

there, for petrol and food, and they told me how to find the cottage. Of course, they thought I was mad, driving in such terrible weather.'

'You were!' she retorted, and he eyed her quizzically.

'What about you? Why on earth are you here, at this time of year?'

She explained about the building work which had been done, and why her mother had wanted to know the cottage had been left in good condition, and he gave her a cynical look.

'So while she's on holiday in sunny Italy you had to drive all the way down here, in a blizzard?'

'She isn't on holiday!'

'Why is she in Italy, then?'

She hesitated. 'Business.' She wasn't going to tell him about Giorgio's problems; he would only leap to the conclusion that the poor man had brought them on himself.

His black brows flickered upwards in wry comment. 'It's quite incredible to think of her turning into a successful busineswoman. I remember her as a quiet little woman always in the background. It amazed me when she ran off with that Italian. My father always thought she would come back—he said it was just a middle-aged fling.'

Juliet's blue eyes glittered with anger. 'Giorgio was the best thing that ever happened to my mother, and I don't blame her for grabbing him after years of living "in the background", as you put it. Why do you think she was so quiet? Living with my father was slowly killing her. She always says it was like living on a desert island alone with someone who didn't seem to notice that she was there. Her natural personality was bubbly and lively, but my father was so withdrawn that he managed to smother her.'

He leaned back in his chair, a hand roughly thrust through his hair, grimacing. 'Yes, your father's a hard man to live with, I can believe that.' He stared challengingly over the table. 'Don't you want to hear how he is?'

She met his grey eyes, her chin up. 'Did he send me any message?'

He shook his head, still watching her.

There was bleakness in her face. 'Well, I don't want to hear about him, either. The day I left Chantries I made up my mind to forget he existed.'

Simeon's sharp eyes probed her features like a lancet, looking for some weak point, then he shrugged. 'He's pretty fit, actually. The life he leads, I suppose. He hates my guts, of course, and doesn't bother to hide it. Oh, he takes any order I give him, without a word, and if we pass each other he gives me a nod, but somehow he makes it clear that he blames me for everything.'

'That makes two of us, then,' she muttered, looking down.

'What?'

His voice made her jump, but she stubbornly repeated what she had said, in a louder voice.

'You blame me?' he snarled, then laughed in a harsh, unamused way. 'How like a woman. It couldn't be your fault, could it? You didn't throw yourself at me, day after day? You didn't make it very plain what you wanted——'

'I didn't know what I was doing—I was too young,' she defended. She had been crazy about him, the wild, uncontrollable infatuation of first love, her mind and heart possessed by a desire she had never felt before, and hadn't known how to handle. If he had repulsed her she would never have let it show so openly, though. She had been much too shy and unsure of herself. Simeon could have averted what happened. He could have discouraged her, gently. But he hadn't. On the contrary, he had let her believe that he felt the same intense attraction.

'That night,' she accused, 'you could have sent me away, but you didn't. You should never have kissed me that night.'

'I kissed you?' he repeated fiercely, and her colour burnt higher.

'Well, maybe I started to kiss you first, but you didn't have to kiss me back. You weren't a teenager, you were an adult man.'

'And I was the one who had to pay,' he ground out. 'They made me marry you, remember. It was a high price to pay for a few kisses.'

She laughed bitterly. 'Oh, I remember. And to get your own back, you made *me* pay on our wedding night, didn't you?'

Dark colour swept up his face, his hands clenched into fists. For a second she tensed, afraid that Simeon might lose control. After all, he had lost control on their wedding night.

'I was angrier than I had ever been in my life before,' he muttered, his face moody.

'You didn't have to be so brutal!' she accused, and his eyes flashed.

'Juliet, heaven help me, if you don't stop saying things like that I'll——'

'What? Hit me?' she interrupted and he breathed audibly, staring at her.

'I've never gone in for hitting women, although for you I might make an exception! If I was less than gentle with you that night it was because I was furious at being forced into marrying you!'

She bit down on her lip, flinching, and he caught that reaction and frowningly sighed.

'I'm sorry, Juliet, but surely now you can see why I felt that way? You're not a schoolgirl any more. If your father hadn't made me feel so guilty, practically accusing me of rape, calling you vile names... my God, what else could I do but say I'd marry you? And then I felt I'd been a fool, I felt trapped. I kept trying to think of a way out, but there was none. My father and your father had made up their minds by then—even if I could have convinced my own father that you were still a virgin, that I'd never had you, your father was going to insist on the marriage. Well, that was what I believed, and I still think his pride would have made it too hard for him to back down. I had to go through with it.'

'Don't talk about it any more!' she broke out, shivering. Simeon was right; she could understand how he had felt—maybe she had even felt the same way? Her father had destroyed something that night. The distaste in his face had made her ashamed, her love for Simeon had turned sour and shrivelled as she faced her father's accusing eyes. She had tried to convince herself that she was happy to be marrying him, that it was her dream come true, but even before he was so cruel to her on their wedding night she had been dreading the future.

'We have to talk about it sooner or later!' Simeon snapped. 'What happened that night made my father change his will, and wrecked my life!'

'What do you think it did to mine?' she retorted.

He fell silent, then abruptly got up from the table, and began to clear the breakfast things.

Relieved, she began to help him carry them into the kitchen and stack the dishwasher. When everything was tidy, Simeon wandered around the sitting-room looking at the photos and ornaments, his face thoughtful. She watched him uneasily, curled up like a small, nervous cat in a deep armchair, her legs under her, wondering what he was thinking and what on earth to say to get through to him that he had to leave. A glance at the window told her that the snow was still blowing in the wind she could hear howling around the house. There was no chance of being able to get away for hours yet, but she was nervous of being here alone with him.

'You seem to have had a pretty successful life since I last saw you, in fact,' he drily commented at last, throwing himself down on the couch beside her chair, and staring at her with his hands linked behind his head. 'Running away to join your mother gave you a new start. I should have gone away, too, but I felt I couldn't just walk out on my father. I had to stay and face the music. It wasn't easy, believe, me.' His mouth twisted. 'Especially with your father treating me like a pariah. He was at my father's funeral, and he didn't speak to me, even then, just walked away afterwards.'

'I don't know how my mother stood it for as long as she did,' Juliet said absently, noticing how the cold sunlight gleamed on his thick black hair. There were one or two silvery hairs among them now, she suddenly saw for the first time. Time was catching up with him. He would be forty in a few years. It seemed incredible.

'She must have loved him once,' said Simeon.

'Only because he was so unlike anyone she had ever met,' Juliet said. 'She told me once—she married him because he was so hard to fathom, silent and mysterious, a mystery man. She thought she would be the one to get past his wall of silence, she would understand him—but she didn't. What she didn't realise was that he didn't need her, need anyone. I wonder what would have happened to her if she hadn't met Giorgio. He's a lovely man, he makes her so happy. She's quite different. You wouldn't know her. They've built up a very successful business together. They are real partners, they make all the decisions together, see each other all day, work happily together. It's all the complete opposite of her years with my father.'

'I read an article about them once,' he surprised her by saying. 'They were opening a new store in Manchester, and there was a photo of them. I recognised your mother, even though she had changed so much. She looked terrific. I can see what you mean; she looked as if she was happy. I had had no idea how successful they were, until then. You were mentioned—"their daughter, Juliet, who works for the company in London". An elegant brunette, they called you.' His eyes flickered over her in gleaming assessment. 'Elegant? Hmm...not quite, not this morning.'

Because of the freezing weather, she had put on the warmest clothes she had with her; they had been left behind that autumn, after her last visit, when she had helped to paint the old barn behind the cottage. She hadn't bothered to pack these things up afterwards, just washed them and put them into a drawer, where she had found them that morning, smelling slightly of a lavender-perfumed sachet she had packed in with them: old, well-washed jeans, a yellow-striped man's shirt, from Italy, which she had borrowed years ago from Giorgio, during a phase when she had loved to wear men's shirts, waistcoats and jackets, and a comfortably thick yellow lambswool riding sweater. She had had another motive for picking this outfit. These were the least attractive clothes she had with her. She was wearing them as an armour against Simeon.

'You look down-to-earth, practical and ready for whatever comes,' he said, and she didn't think he was flattering her. Perhaps he had even guessed she had worn these clothes to put him off. He paused, watching her, then asked softly, 'Are you?' and she stared, confused.

'Am I what?'

'Ready for whatever comes,' he said and watched with a smile as a flush crept up her face. 'You know, I hardly recognise you,' he suddenly said. 'If I'd walked past you in the street I probably wouldn't have known you.'

'You never did,' she said, head lowered, mouth stubborn. 'Any more than you knew my mother.'

'Well, here we are, quite alone—this time we will get to know each other.' He got up and she went into a panic and scrambled up, too, knocking over her chair.

'Don't touch me!' She had been pushing his threat to the back of her mind, trying to convince herself that he hadn't meant what he said, but fear suddenly swamped her mind and she began to tremble violently. 'I couldn't bear it if you touched me,' she whispered, staring at him.

'You'll have to bear it,' Simeon said in a low, harsh voice, and his eyes held a disturbing insistence which warned her that he meant precisely what he said.

## CHAPTER FOUR

'I'M GOING for a walk,' Juliet said desperately, heading for the door, and hoping he wouldn't stop her.

He didn't. He came after her in long, unhurried strides. 'Good idea. It seems to have stopped snowing and the sky is as blue as your eyes.'

She blinked, taken aback by the simile, but didn't risk looking at him, just grabbed her sheepskin coat from the cupboard in the little hallway, buttoned herself into it, found some shabby old boots, and put on Fair Isle woolen gloves and a matching woollen hood which she had bought on a trip to Scotland with her mother and Giorgio several years ago, and which she kept here in Cornwall because they were the perfect things to wear on long walks across the moor on cold days.

She gave Simeon a glance, noting that he had put on his leather jacket, those high black leather boots which looked like the sort of boots motorcyclists wore, and leather gloves. Offhandedly, she said, 'There are some warm scarves in here, if you'd like to borrow one.' She pulled out a long red wollen one which belonged to Giorgio.

'Thanks,' Simeon said, bending his head. 'Put it on for me, would you, please?'

She hesitated, then quickly threw it round his neck, trying not to touch him, but in her haste her fingers brushed his cheek and she only just managed not to give a cry of shock at the electric buzz that brief contact gave her. He looked down at her with a crooked little smile.

'Thank you.'

She quickly turned away and pulled open the door and they both looked out, their eyes narrowed against the brilliance of sunlight reflected on mirror-like snow. The wind had dropped; it was nowhere near so cold. The landscape looked marvellous; great, rolling acres of untrodden snow, white and dazzling under that blue sky. It was so beautiful it caught the breath, but it was so empty. Not another house or human being in sight. Juliet stared at that emptiness, biting her lip.

'Changed your mind? It is cold!' said Simeon drily, and she gave him a resentful look, banging the door shut behind her.

'Certainly not.' She began to walk briskly and he fell in beside her, easily keeping step because his legs were so much longer than hers. She saw his black shadow moving on the glassy snow beside her own, fantastical, elongated, rather disturbing in all that empty landscape, as though he haunted her. Or hunted her, she thought, with an inward shudder.

'Did you really want to cross the moor? Remember, heather isn't easy stuff to walk through,' she said, being deliberately patronising.

He gave her a glinting smile, aware of the challenge. 'Oh, I expect I can cope.'

'OK, don't say I didn't warn you,' she said sweetly, and they turned off the road on to the open

moorland, their pace slowing once they were struggling through snow-covered heather, then they came
out on to a grassy slope which the snow had turned
into a frozen slide. Juliet felt her feet go from under
her, and careered downwards with a cry, her arms
flailing in an attempt to retrieve her balance. She
landed with a thump on her behind, and heard
Simeon laughing above her.

So he thought that was funny, did he? She felt
stupid, especially after warning him against the
moor, and that made her aggressive. Very flushed,
her bones aching from the jar of the fall, she
scooped up two handfuls of snow, firmed them into
a ball and turned to hurl it in his direction.

She got a direct hit, right on his head, the black
hair suddenly dusted with powdery snow, and sat,
open-mouthed with surprise, because she had never
been a particularly good shot. She should have got
up and run on, because sitting there she was a
perfect target, and Simeon moved faster than a
rattlesnake.

He bent, straightened, and a second later a
snowball hit her and snow showered around her.
She grabbed another handful herself, and leapt to
her feet, firing off her ammunition before she took
to her heels. She heard Simeon set off in pursuit,
and ran faster, her breathing rough and ragged in
her throat. It was only a game—but that wasn't
how it felt to her.

He caught her a moment later, both arms going
round her, and she struggled wildly, panic in her
face. 'Let go!' she cried, her body arching away

from him as far as it could while he held it in the
powerful circle of his arms.

'Stop fighting it,' he murmured, looking down
at her, his grey eyes very bright and watchful, and
despite her fear she noticed that he had not said
'Stop fighting me', and that that was deliberate.
'Stop fighting *it*,' he had said, because he was
hinting that she felt some drag of attraction, that
she wanted him to kiss her even though she resisted.

'I don't want it,' she lied, staring at his mouth
with a confused feeling. She didn't know what to
call it, only that it couldn't be desire, yet her mouth
had gone dry and she felt strangely dizzy. 'No,' she
tried to say, but her lips moved without making any
sound, while he watched them intently, as if lip-
reading.

'Yes,' he whispered, and then his gloved hands
came up to frame her face between their palms.

She couldn't escape his mouth—he held her head
just where he wanted it. His lips were icy with snow
when they touched hers at first, and she gave a little
indrawn gasp. As her lips parted in that involuntary sound Simeon's kiss deepened, grew fierce,
invading her mouth, forcing back her head so that
she had to grab him to keep her balance, her hands
gripping his wide shoulders. She shut her eyes because the blue sky seemed to be spinning above her
and her head was swimming too. His mouth moved
in hot demand and she helplessly met it, hanging
on to him, her body trembling, no longer even
making a pretence of fighting. She had had a
number of boyfriends over the past eight years, but

none of them had ever made her go weak at the knees with one kiss.

It was Simeon who broke off the kiss, just as it had been Simeon who began it. He lifted his head and she felt him looking down at her while she clung to his shoulders, shaking, her eyes closed and her lips burning from the demands he had made on them.

'Next time you're tempted to chuck things at me, remember what the consequences are likely to be, and think again,' he said softly, with mockery, and her eyes flew open, her face very flushed as she met his amused gaze.

'Thanks for the tip! I won't forget,' she said furiously. 'I certainly wouldn't want that to happen again!'

His eyes taunted her. 'Sure about that? I got the impression you were enjoying it.'

'Certain!' she snapped, even angrier because he was quite right and the last thing she wanted was for him to realise he could get her that way. Physically, he attracted her, she couldn't deny it even to herself, but that meant nothing. Her body could make dangerous mistakes, her body craved pleasure, was easily tempted—her mind was a much more reliable guide.

She pulled away from him, avoiding his shrewd, narrowed eyes, and began to walk fast, back towards the cottage, aware after a pause that Simeon was following her, his booted feet crunching on the snow. Ahead of her stretched the double line of footprints, hers and Simeon's, showing the way they had come. A strange sensation hit her, a superstitious quiver along her spine while she stared as if at an omen, and tried to avoid crossing that track.

'Why don't you walk in our footsteps, like King Wenceslas?' Simeon asked behind her, but she pretended not to hear, and went on walking a little to one side of the line.

Simeon halted a moment later. She didn't look back, just plodded on, until he called out to her, 'Look, just coming over those pines...a hawk...what is it, can you see? Sparrowhawk?'

Juliet paused, shading her eyes with one hand while she stared at the blue sky. A dark shape was skating on the wind, pinions spread, but so far away that she couldn't identify it positively.

'I thought I caught a flash of white on the rump,' Simeon said.

'That would be a sparrowhawk,' she agreed, watching to see if she could see the tell-tale blur of white, but at that moment the hawk swooped in descent and they lost it until it soared upward again, carrying something between its talons. Juliet gave a short sigh. 'He's killed.'

Simeon caught up with her, giving her averted profile a hard stare. 'He has to kill to live,' he reminded.

'I know,' she snapped, glaring. 'You were always telling me that when I was small. I hated it then, I hate it now.'

His face was unyielding, a hard mask. 'Hate it or not, it's the way the world works, and there's nothing you can do about that, Juliet.'

'I don't have to like it,' she said confusedly, her mind filled with the image of something small and soft, helplessly struggling against the cruel talons carrying it away.

Simeon caught hold of her chin and lifted her face, his cold grey eyes hunting over it remorselessly while she tried to hide what she was thinking. 'Nature is "red in tooth and claw",' he said coolly. 'You can't change that, and fighting it would only lead to disaster.'

She looked angrily into his eyes, her face obstinate. They weren't only talking about the hawk and its prey, and they both knew it. 'It's cruel,' she said and he shrugged.

'Hawks are rare and beautiful birds, but nature did not intend them to be vegetarians. You can't change the law of their nature, Juliet. They have to be ruthless or die.'

He had to be ruthless or lose Chantries, he was telling her, and his hard mouth and merciless eyes warned her against trying to escape the fate he had planned for her.

'No!' she cried out in protest, pulling her head free and turning to run. Simeon let her go, and didn't even try to catch up with her. Breathlessly stumbling over the deep snow, her legs shaky under her, she heard his unhurried footsteps on her heels, always coming after her, not to be shaken off, as certain as death, making her heart knock like a premonition against her ribs.

Reaching the cottage at last, she unlocked the front door and stamped the snow off her boots outside before she entered. She left her boots on the doormat in the hall, pulled off her coat and hood, and her warm Fair Isle gloves, before hurrying into the kitchen to put on the coffee percolator.

She heard the sound of Simeon scraping snow off his own boots, and then the slam of the front door as he came inside. That bang seemed to echo in her head, shutting them in together, shutting out the world.

Once the coffee was on the stove, she ran upstairs to the bathroom, calling out, 'The coffee is on!'

'Can I help?' Simeon asked from the hall.

'You could put out the cups,' she replied casually, without looking back down at him.

Washing her hands a few moments later, she stared at her reflection in the mirror above the basin. Her skin was glowing a warm pink from the cold air and exercise, and her eyes were bright, as if with fever. She eyed herself with alarm and anxiety.

He had only been here a few hours, and already he had done something drastic to her. She hadn't looked like that before.

Like what? she asked herself angrily, drying her hands roughly with a peach-coloured hand towel. Like what, for heaven's sake? What *did* she look like? What was she afraid of? Simeon wouldn't . . . well, he wouldn't . . . It was hard even to put her worst fears into words. She hesitated even to think it, but she had to. Simeon wouldn't use force.

She met her own eyes in the mirror again, and glared at herself. No, that was unthinkable. Simeon wouldn't. Whatever else he might be capable of, that was not possible. She was certain that he wsn't the type to rape a woman.

But that didn't make her feel any better, any less nervous, because that was not what she was afraid of, was it? What was really bothering her was that Simeon might not even need to use force. Force wasn't going to come into his strategy. She had been given a glimpse of how he meant to get his own way, and she was scared stiff now. He meant to seduce her. And he might well do it.

Look at you! she said to her reflection, her blue eyes accusing. Well, just look at you! One kiss and he sends you into a daze, your knees give way and you look feverish.

What is going to happen when he turns on the heat? As he will, make no mistake about it. He has come here determined to get you into bed, and you can't get away, so what are you going to do? How are you going to keep him at arm's length?

She had so many questions—but not a single answer.

Turning away with a helpless sigh, she reluctantly made her way downstairs. If only the cottage were not so remote. Now that the snow had stopped, the snow ploughs would be out, clearing the main roads, but having been out for that walk she knew just how deep the snow was, and there was no chance of her car making it to the main road. She was a prisoner here, with Simeon, for the moment. She had to think of some way of dealing with him, but she hadn't a clue how.

Just as she reached the hall, the phone began to ring, making her jump.

'Shall I get it?' called Simeon from the kitchen, and alarm shot through her.

'No, that's OK, I will,' she hurriedly shouted back, running to snatch up the phone in the sitting-room. It was probably her mother with the latest news of Giorgio, and she certainly didn't want her mother to hear Simeon's voice and start putting two and two together and making a hundred and three.

Simeon appeared in the doorway and watched her, his grey eyes narrow and alert. She turned her back to hide her expression.

'Hello?' she said, expecting her mother's voice.

'So you did go,' said a curt male voice, and for a moment she couldn't even place it, so much had happened since she left London. 'I didn't really believe you meant it,' the angry voice added, and that was when his identity dawned and she took a deep breath.

'Oh . . . Adam . . .'

She felt Simeon move closer, his whole attention on her.

'Will you be back by tonight?' Adam asked in a way which threatened and yet had a pleading note.

'I'm sorry,' she said, wishing Simeon would go away, would stop eavesdropping and watching her. It was hard enough to talk to Adam without having an audience.

'Julie!' Adam broke out. 'You know how important this is to me! Don't be stubborn—you can get back if you leave now.'

'Isn't it snowing in London? It snowed all night here—the roads are totally blocked, I couldn't possibly get back, even if I set out right now.'

Adam said something violent, so loudly that she sensed Simeon picking the words up. She shot him a look over her shoulder and found him far too close, and listening intently. She gave him a furious stare, frowning, and waved him away with a peremptory hand. He had no right to listen in to her private calls.

He didn't move, just lounged negligently against the wall nearby, his expression bland.

Turning away, she said softly into the phone, 'I'm really sorry, Adam, I'd get back if I could.' And because Simeon was listening, she went on, 'I wish I hadn't come, I wish I was back in London with you, safe and sound.' She meant it, too, her voice husky with sincerity, although for very different reasons than those she was implying, not that it mattered, because Adam was too angry to pick up any nuances in her tone.

'It's a bit late for regrets now, though, isn't it?' he snapped. 'What am I supposed to do? I can't go to this affair alone—I have to take a partner.'

'Yes, I know, I'm sorry, Adam.' She felt Simeon's eyes boring a hole into the back of her head and fumed. Why didn't he have the decency to go away?

'Sorry? You walk out on me at a time when I really need you, for no important reason, either, and then say you're sorry?' Adam was shouting now, almost deafening her, and she held the phone a little away from ear.

A second later it was snatched from her hand, and she gave a gasp of shock as she looked up at Simeon's taut face.

'That's enough,' he snarled into the phone while Juliet desperately tried to take it back from him, only to be held off by one hand. 'I won't have any man shouting at my wife down a phone. So clear off.'

She heard the confused sound of Adam reacting to the terse male voice, then Simeon slammed the phone down and cut him off.

'You...' Juliet stammered, so angry she couldn't speak. 'You...'

Simeon stared down at her, his long, lean body very still, but his face grim. 'All right, who is he?' he asked, his lips barely parting to let the sound out.

'You had no right to do that!' seethed Juliet, trembling with resentment.

'Did he have a right to yell at you down a phone?' Simeon snapped, his eyes bleak.

'If I'd wanted to hang up on him, I would have done!' she threw back, glaring up at him.

Simeon bit out, 'So why didn't you? Is he your lover?'

Her colour rose even higher, but she held his contemptuous stare, throwing back that contempt at him. 'If he is, that's my business, not yours!'

Violence glittered in the grey eyes, and he grabbed her by the shoulders, shaking her. 'Is he? Tell me, damn you!'

'I'm not telling you anything!'

'You will!' There was threat in his voice, but she defied him, her chin lifted and her blue eyes obstinate.

'Nothing would make me!'

'No?' he said tersely, and a shudder of panic ran through her at something in his hard face.

He began to pull her towards him, his strength more than a match for her, but then the phone began to ring again and he swore under his breath, one hand immediately moving to snatch the phone up.

'Yes?' he grated.

'Give me that phone,' Juliet said, struggling to take it, but Simeon shifted, his head averted so that she couldn't quite reach.

She heard Adam loudly demand, 'Who is that?'

'I'm her husband. Don't ring again, because I shall just hang up on you,' Simeon said and slammed the phone down again, cutting off Adam's angry spluttering.

Juliet wanted to hit Simeon—she was so angry she was shaking with it, muttering hoarsely. 'How dare you? Who do you think you are? You're...' Words jammed up in her brain, she couldn't form sentences properly, she was so furious. She just spat out words incoherently, glaring up at him with enraged blue eyes. 'High-handed, arrogant...the most...interfering, insolent, laying down the law... You force your way back into my life and start trying to dictate to me! I'm not putting up with it.'

'Shut up!' Simeon suddenly bit out, and pulled her violently towards him, her writhing body helpless against his powerful grip.

When he had kissed her earlier, out on the snowy moorland, his mouth had been quite gentle at first before heat came into the kiss, but this time his mouth was cruel, angry, not caring if it hurt, and she fought against him, trying to pull her head away.

In her struggle, she lost her balance and began to fall, letting herself go in the hope of escaping, but he came with her, holding on to her, although he had stopped kissing her, and they landed on the couch, then rolled, still struggling, on to the floor.

Juliet found herself lying on top of him, her eyes inches away from his. She looked away, and tried to get up but Simeon rolled her deftly over until she was underneath, and he was on top, his powerful body anchoring her down. His weight seemed to crush all the breath out of her body. She lay very still, her skin suddenly pale, pulled tight over her cheekbones, her blue eyes as open as they could stretch, staring up at him in fear.

He stared down at her, lying equally still, hardly seeming to breathe, either. In the charged silence she heard the deep hammer-beat of his heart and hardly knowing what she was doing she put a shaky hand on his deep chest to feel the vibration under her palm while he watched her.

His mouth twisted. 'You can't help it, can you?'

'Can't help what?' She was moved by the sensation of having that heartbeat throbbing into her own body through her palm. Simeon was so alive, so vital. She couldn't imagine that heart ever stopping; a man with a heartbeat like that would live for ever, she thought, half smiling.

'Flirting, being provocative,' he accused, and she snatched her hand away.

'I wasn't!'

'What were you doing, then?' He picked up her hand and put it back on his chest, held it there, staring into her eyes. 'What else was that, but pure provocation? You touched me of your own accord, don't pretend you didn't, and that's how it happened in the first place, and you know it. That summer, it wasn't me who did the chasing—it was you.'

Her eyes fell, she bit her lip. It was true, she couldn't deny it, and she had felt guilty about the consequences ever since. Simeon certainly hadn't chased her; at first he had been amused, quite indulgent, still thinking of her as a child. He had let her tag along with him when he went for walks or played tennis or swam, but there had been no shadow of sexual interest in his behaviour. He had acted like a friendly big brother, which was not what she had wanted at all, and her pride had been galled.

She had been seventeen—a woman, in her own eyes, and the sea tides of adult sexuality had been flowing back and forth in her veins, making her confused and unsure of herself. She acted and reacted without knowing quite what she was doing; it was all instinctive, involuntary.

Oh, yes, she had flirted with him, become provocative and inviting, but she had been playing at it, as a kitten with a ball of wool played at making its first kill. Her real mistake, her folly, had been in picking someone outside her own age-group to experiment with—if she had chosen a boy of seventeen it would have been an exciting summer romance which could have ended gently, but on which one could have looked back with pleasure all one's life. It wouldn't have wrecked two lives.

But she hadn't been interested in boys. Maybe she had always liked Simeon a lot—who could say? She only knew how she had felt that summer; the wild, burning excitement, the drag of need in her body.

So she had made him look at her in a very different way. She had made him see her as a woman. Passion had given her cunning, taught her a woman's skills. She had left the top buttons of her shirts undone, giving glimpses of her small, high breasts; she had bought some new clothes which had changed her whole appearance, made her suddenly very grown-up. Very short shorts, a silky, clinging dress to dance in, a very revealing bikini, in which she had lain about in the sun, her slender little body becoming golden brown and, she hoped, sexy.

Most of all, she had looked at Simeon through her lashes with smouldering invitation, and after a while he had stopped looking amused and started looking back at her in a way that had sent feverish shivers through her whole body.

'Admit it,' Simeon said now, his voice biting, and she gave a long sigh.

'What do you want me to say—that I'm sorry? I am, but that doesn't change anything, does it? OK, I had a crush on you, and I flirted with you, and it all ended badly, but I didn't know what I was doing, none of it was intentional and it was all so long ago. You should have divorced me years ago, married again, then your father wouldn't have made that stupid will.'

'But he did, and we aren't divorced, we're still married, and you are going to give me a child to inherit Chantries.' His voice was brusque—it hit her like a blow.

She trembled, her blue eyes opening wide again, her lips parting on a gasp of rejection. 'No, I won't!'

He stared at her mouth, his grey eyes cruel and insistent. 'You will,' he assured her, his head coming closer, his mouth slowly lowering towards her own.

'No,' she whispered, staring at his mouth and shaking. The hard-cut lines of it fascinated her; there was generosity there, and sexual promise, but held under rein, firmly controlled. It was almost touching her lips now, and the beat of her heart deafened her.

Then the phone began to ring again and Simeon swore, his head lifting, his face darkening with irritation.

'Not him again! Doesn't he know when to give up?'

She laughed almost hysterically. 'No, giving up isn't something Adam is good at. He likes to win.'

She got a hard stare, a grim frown. 'Well, this time he isn't going to, so he had better get used to the idea.'

The ringing went on and on, seeming to get shriller by the minute. 'We must answer it,' Juliet said, and Simeon angrily got up and strode to the phone.

'Right,' he began, while Juliet was getting to her feet. 'Look here, you...'

Then his voice broke off and he listened, his mouth twisting, before turning to hold out the phone to her.

She had an instant's premonition and groaned as she ran to take the phone from him.

'It's your mother,' he told her, quite unnecessarily, because she had known that when she saw his expression change.

'Hello, Mum,' she said huskily and almost held the phone away from her ear as Shirley Mendelli burst out with agitated questions which she did not give Juliet time to answer before gabbling another one.

'Who was that? What's going on? Darling, is something wrong? Why is there a man with you at the cottage? It isn't Adam, I would know his voice and this is quite different. Nasty, I'd even say threatening, the way he snarled at me just now...who is it? And why did he answer the phone that way? Julie, are you all right? Would you like me to ring the police, or——'

'Mum! Mum!' Juliet broke in on her loudly, and at last Shirley stopped and drew breath. 'Mum,' Juliet said with a sigh, 'it's Simeon——'

'Simeon?' repeated her mother blankly, then, with astonishment, 'Simeon? Do you mean Simeon Gerard? Robert's son?'

'Yes...'

'What on earth is he doing there? I haven't heard anything about that family for years. I didn't know you still kept in touch, you've never mentioned him to me. I never liked him much, he was such an arrogant boy—I don't suppose he's changed.'

'Not much,' Juliet admitted wryly, giving Simeon a brief, sideways glance. 'Mum, he brought me some sad news——'

'Your father?' Shirley's voice changed, sharpened.

'No, his,' Juliet said quickly. 'He died a few weeks ago.'

'Oh, I'm sorry, Robert was a nice man,' her mother said soberly.

'Yes,' Juliet agreed, then changed the subject. 'Why did you ring, though, Mum? Anything wrong? How's Giorgio?'

'Oh, he's fine, there's nothing wrong here, but I rang London just now and heard about the weather down in Cornwall, so I was worried about you. Is it the snow really heavy there? Will you be able to drive back to London today? Now, I don't want you killing yourself trying to drive on icy roads, just to get back to work, darling.'

'I couldn't if I wanted to,' Juliet said heavily. 'The roads are completely blocked around here for the moment. We're hoping the snow ploughs will be able to get out and clear the main roads but unless the weather changes overnight I shan't be able to get back to London for a while, but I shall ring the office in the morning and tell Helen to hold the fort.'

'Your secretary can't run the business, though,' Shirley said. 'I had better fly back.'

'Wait until tomorrow morning, and check with me again, Mum,' Juliet said firmly. 'If I can get

back to London, somehow, without killing myself,
I promise you, I will. You stay there with Giorgio.
How is he now?'

Shirley sighed. 'Calmer, thank heavens. Poor
darling. But, Julie, don't you think I ought to come
back, just in case...?'

'No, I think your place is with Giorgio, and,
anyway, there's nothing urgent happening for a few
days. Helen can cope, and I am sure I'll be able to
get back to London somehow. I can always take a
train.' If I can get as far as the nearest railway
station, seven miles away, she thought wryly, but
didn't say to her mother.

Shirley suddenly asked, 'But why did Simeon
Gerard come all the way to Cornwall to tell you
that his father was dead, darling? And why was he
so nasty when he answered the phone just now?
Really, he scared the life out of me—I thought I'd
got a wrong number for a minute.'

'Oh, well,' Juliet said, desperately thinking of
some excuse without explaining how angry Adam
was because she knew that her mother would feel
guilty if she knew that he resented Juliet coming
down to Cornwall to check up on the cottage. 'Well,
you see, I'd had a couple of funny phone
calls... you know the sort, heavy breathing.'

'Oh, how frightening!' Shirley gave an audible
shudder. 'Ugh...I am sorry, darling. But how lucky
Simeon turned up this morning and could answer
the phone instead of you! Knowing there's a man
there should put a stop to that! Did you ring the
police? Oh, you should, Julie. He may be
dangerous.'

'OK, Mum,' Juliet said.

'You still haven't explained why Simeon came all that way, though,' remembered Shirley. 'Were you mentioned in the will? You aren't going to be very rich, are you?'

'Afraid not, nothing so exciting,' Juliet casually said. 'But I am mentioned in the will, and that is why Simeon came down here. Just something Robert wanted me to do... I'll tell you all about it later—this call must be costing a fortune. Keep in touch, Mum, love to Giorgio.'

'Bye, darling,' Shirley said, and Juliet hung up.

She turned to face Simeon, who was eying her with dry mockery. 'So,' he said. 'You didn't have the nerve to tell her the truth. Does she even know we're married?'

She lifted her chin with defiance. 'No, and I'd rather she never found out, I don't want anyone to know. What I want is for you to divorce me——'

'After you've had my child,' he promised, and his face was relentless.

# CHAPTER FIVE

Juliet stood there looking at Simeon dumbly, wondering how she was going to make him understand that she couldn't, it was impossible, the very idea made her blood run cold; and he watched her—without expression now, his grey eyes cool and alert.

Then his face changed and he groaned. 'The coffee! I switched it off and poured two cups.'

She had forgotten the coffee too. They both ran for the kitchen, but the coffee in the cups was cold, and there wasn't enough left in the percolator to make two good cups.

'I'll make some more,' Juliet said but Simeon shook his head, glancing at the kitchen clock.

'I'll have instant—I'm quite happy with that, especially as it is almost lunchtime.' He filled the kettle and put it on and found a jar of instant coffee granules in a cupboard.

'Lunchtime?' She looked at the clock, too, amazed to see that he was right. It was almost one o'clock, and as soon as she realised that she began to feel hungry. 'What shall we have?' she thought aloud, opening cupboards and looking in the fridge. There wasn't that much choice. She would have to fall back on something from her stock cupboard, and a tin or two. 'How do you feel about rice or spaghetti with a tomato sauce?' she asked him and he shrugged.

'Fine with me. There are some mushrooms left, too, and I bought onions.'

'Then we're in business,' she said, and began to prepare the meal while Simeon made the coffee and sat down at the table with his, apparently to watch her work. Blandly, Juliet asked, 'Can you chop onions, or do they make you cry?'

'Nothing makes me cry,' he said, grinning at her, and she wondered how true that was. It could be, from what she knew of him—he seemed impervious enough to her. But what did anyone know about another human being? He could get angry, but could he be hurt?

She handed him a kitchen knife and a large onion, and went to look for a pan in which to make the sauce while the water for the spaghetti boiled.

When she looked round, a pan in her hand, Simeon was already chopping away with quick, deft movements.

'You've done that before,' she said, and he nodded without looking up, his attention on what he was doing.

'I cook for myself, although I have someone in to do the cleaning. I stick to plain cooking, mostly—preferably something I can grill or leave to cook in the oven all day while I'm out. Casseroles, or steak, or maybe fish. I bake potatoes in the oven, too, or make a salad.'

'Good heavens, chef of the year,' she mocked, and he laughed.

'Well, I did eat out a lot at one time, but that gets boring, and once a woman starts cooking for a man she gets ideas.'

He had finished; there was a neat little pile of chopped onion on the wooden board. He turned to ask, 'What about the mushrooms?'

'I'll wash them and just halve them,' she said, wondering how many women had offered to cook for him over the past eight years. He was a sexy man, no denying that; there must have been plenty of women buzzing around that particular honey-pot, and she felt a niggling little jab under her ribs at the images forming in her head. Sharply she told herself that it was none of her business; she wasn't a lovestruck teenager any more, she was a sane, sensible woman and Simeon Gerard's love-life was his own affair.

The water was boiling—she fed the spaghetti into it, and turned all her attention to making the sauce. Simeon laid the table, and then began opening cupboards and investigating their contents while she worked.

'Look what I found!' he exclaimed, producing a slightly dusty bottle of red wine. 'Nothing exciting, a cheap plonk really, but it should add a little sparkle to the meal.'

Juliet stared doubtfully at the bottle—was it wise to let him drink over lunch? Wine in the middle of the day always made her sleepy—would it have that effect on him? Now, that might be a good idea.

'Fine, will you open it?' she said.

He gave her a quick, dry glance, and she wondered if he had read her mind, but he made no comment, just set about finding a corkscrew and opening the wine, which he tasted himself and pronounced drinkable.

Juliet concentrated on her sauce, the kitchen filling with a rich aroma of tomato and onion, then she drained the spaghetti and divided it between the two plates waiting for it, adding the sauce on top. Simeon had poured them each a glass; there hadn't been time to let the wine reach room temperature but they warmed their glasses in their hands before drinking, and it wasn't at all bad, with the spaghetti, although Juliet merely sipped hers.

She watched through her lashes while Simeon drank several glasses, hoping it would make him lethargic for the rest of the afternoon. So far it didn't seem to be having any effect at all.

'I enjoyed that,' he said, as he ate the last mouthful of the meal. 'You're a good cook.'

'Anyone can cook spaghetti,' she disclaimed.

'You must teach me, then. It looked easy enough.' He got up, clearing the plates from the table, but put a restraining hand on her shoulder as she moved to rise. 'No, I'll make the coffee. You sit there and admire my technique.'

She relaxed, smiling, and watched him operate. It was an object lesson in economy of effort, and it told her a lot about him. He dealt with the coffee first, and only when that was percolating did he put the plates and cutlery into the dishwasher, then lay out a tray for the coffee, after which he washed up the saucepans by hand and left them to drain on the draining-board. He moved swiftly and neatly, and she felt a little shiver run down her spine, because the man was far too organised—he worked things out before he acted, he had it all planned like a military operation, and that cool, logical brain frightened her.

'Shall we drink our coffee in the sitting-room? It would be more comfortable,' he suggested, and before she could argue he had carried the tray out of the kitchen, leaving her with nothing to do but follow him.

He placed the tray on the low coffee-table and gestured to her to seat herself on the couch, but Juliet didn't trust him, so she chose a chair.

He threw her a mocking little smile, commenting on her wariness without a word, then he sat down on the couch and said, 'Would you pour the coffee, please?'

She hesitated, biting her lip, because to do so she had to get up again, and cross over to him, but she could hardly refuse, so she obeyed and poured coffee into both cups, offered him sugar and milk, then handed him his cup before picking up her own.

He caught her other hand as she straightened. 'Sit here.'

She gave him a derisive glance, shaking her head. 'I'd feel safer over there,' she bluntly said, and he laughed.

'Do I bother you that much?'

The soft implications of that made her colour rise, because it was too true—he did bother her, increasingly, and the last thing she wanted was for him to know that.

'You don't bother me at all!' she snapped, and his eyes teased.

'Then why are you afraid to sit next to me?'

She crossly said, 'I haven't forgotten the way you behaved an hour ago, you know!'

'I had provocation, don't forget that,' he taunted, but he let go of her and she went hurrying back to her chair.

Simeon drank some coffee, watching her with brooding eyes, and she drank some of her own coffee, feeling nervous. What was on his mind now? Why was he looking at her like that?

'So, tell me about this Adam,' he said abruptly. She almost dropped her cup, hot coffee splashed on her hand and she gave a sharp exclaimation and put the cup down on the floor and rubbed her skin, where it was reddened.

'What have you done to yourself now?' Simeon demanded with impatience, watching. 'Did you scald your hand?'

'No, it's fine now. You just made me jump, suddenly snapping at me like that.'

'I didn't snap, I just asked a simple question,' he drawled. 'And if I'm to judge by your guilty expression and the way you jumped I suppose I got my answer. He is your lover, isn't he?'

She was afraid to answer that, because if he believed Adam to be her lover it might make him back off; surely he would think again if he knew she was involved with somebody else? In any case, she needed some sort of protection against him. She certainly couldn't rely on herself; they had only been here alone together for around twelve hours, and already she knew that her resistance to him was low, to say the least. She must be losing her mind— she had very good reasons for hating and despising him, didn't she? He had made her very unhappy; the memory of their wedding night still hurt if she let herself dwell on it. Even now, at this instant, to give it a passing thought made her flinch inwardly, and yet he only had to move close to her for her whole body to burn with a desire so fierce that it terrified her.

It was a chemical reaction, she kept telling herself, a violent physical attraction to his body, not to the man himself. Simeon Gerard, she hated; but unfortunately her stupid body apparently had no memory—her pulses went into overdrive at the sight of him, her skin craved his touch, her mouth went dry and she trembled.

'I refuse to discuss my private life with you,' she said, her eyes lowered and obstinacy in every line of her.

'So you admit he is your private life, then?' Simeon promptly said. 'How long has it been going on?'

'I've known him for a year or so.'

'Does he work for this shoe store chain your mother and stepfather started? Is he hoping to marry into the family and one day control the store?' His tone was derisive, chilly, and she resented it for Adam.

'No, he's an executive with another company, a much bigger one, and any ambitions Adam has are centred entirely on his own firm. He isn't interested in shoes or selling. He's a company man, he likes working for big international firms, jetting about, having important business meetings...' She broke off, suddenly realising that the portrait of Adam she was painting was not a very flattering one. Simeon met her eyes, his face gleaming with amused irony.

'He sounds fascinating.'

She went pink with temper. 'He's very good-looking, as it happens!'

'Good-looking, but boring,' mused Simeon, but before she could snap back at him that Adam was not boring he added, 'Which company did you say he worked for?'

'I didn't.' But she did tell him then, curtly, and saw that he wasn't impressed. Simeon was no businessman; his whole world had always been centred on Chantries, on farming and forestry, on the life of the countryside in which he had grown up. His interests were those of a countryman: he loved horses and dogs, rode every day, fished in the gentle river which ran through his land, and shot the rabbits which preyed on his fields of grain.

A man like Adam had such very different attitudes—they were poles apart. Adam had grown up in a poor home, with everything to fight for; if he ever met Simeon, he would undoubtedly think that the other man had been born with a silver spoon in his mouth. Adam resented men like that; he met them every day, he had to compete with them in his company, and often lost out to them because of the school they had been to or who they knew. She had often heard Adam complain angrily about the old boy network, the inbuilt bias towards men from a wealthy background.

'We wouldn't have a thing in common,' Simeon thought aloud, and she laughed shortly.

'No.'

'Except you,' he added, and then, 'But I have no intention of sharing you with him. He's out.'

She gasped incredulously. 'I don't believe you said that!'

'I did, and I mean it,' he coolly underlined. 'You won't see him again.'

'You have absolutely no right to give me orders, or tell me who I can see and who I can't. I'll do what I please!' she told him furiously, her face burning.

'No, you'll do what I please,' he drawled, and his grey eyes moved with deliberate slowness over her from her chestnut hair down to her feet, missing out no part of her and sending her heart into her mouth. She felt as if he had touched her and shuddered, then leapt up to flee, to get away as fast as she could from those tormenting eyes.

She expected him to pursue her, but there was no sound of following feet, as she ran through the hall and headed for the stairs and the safety of her bedroom, and her heartbeat slowed a little. It was only as she was on the top stair that she heard him behind her, and looking down she saw him coming up. That sent a wave of panic through her, and she started to rush across the landing, only to trip over her own feet and stumble against the wall. By the time she had recovered her balance Simeon had caught up with her. She felt her feet leave the ground and clutched at him with a cry of alarm.

'What are you doing? Put me down!'

He carried her into the main bedroom, although she fought angrily and uselessly against the strength of his arms, kicking and pummelling him until he put her down on the silk-quilted double bed. She tried to scramble off the other side, but, laughing, he caught her again, his hands closing on her waist. He was like a cruel cat, she thought, playing with a mouse, allowing her to think she might escape only to capture her again. He was on the bed, too, now, pinning her down with an arm over her, one leg moving to anchor her too, and fear almost swamped her mind.

'I hate you!' she cried out, and he laughed again.

'Do you? That *is* going to make this exciting,' he said softly, and her heart plunged in shock. He lowered his mouth and she turned her head aside to evade his kiss. 'You have a lovely neck,' he whispered, kissing it, his lips moving down in silky exploration, and then with another stab of shock she felt him undo the top button of her shirt, then, swiftly, several more with those deft, experienced fingers. She had observed his economy of movement earlier, with alarm, and now she experienced the same dismay.

'Stop that!' she muttered, trying to push his head away. The feel of his hair under her fingertips was too intimate, though; she wanted to stroke it, she felt his vitality sparking between her skin, his hair, which made her swallow and pull her hand away, her heart beating even faster with an explosive mix of desire and rage.

What is happening to me? she thought wildly, and then his mouth was moving down inside her open shirt, against her naked breasts, and she closed her eyes with a sharp, helpless cry of pleasure.

Her hands came up to touch him, too, one plunging into the thick, warm hair, caressing the powerful nape of his neck, while her other moved over his shoulders, down his back, up his chest, exploring his body. She had forgotten all sanity; she had abandoned any idea of fighting him, was given up entirely to the sweet, erotic sensations running through her.

He lifted his head from her breasts and looked down at her, and Juliet's eyes reluctantly opened, dazed by the light. Simeon ran a fingertip over her lips, and they parted for him. Still staring into her passion-darkened blue eyes, he slowly lowered his head and this time she did not try to evade his searching mouth or fight. She arched to meet his kiss, a husky little sound escaping her, and closed her eyes again. This was how she had felt that night, in the orchard, under the stars, before her father had found them and all hell broke loose.

She had forgotten until now exactly how she had felt, how piercing had been the emotion inside her when Simeon had held her in his arms. She sighed heavily against his hungry mouth, her arms around him, her hands moving up and down his back, clenching on him, and he groaned with husky intensity.

'Juliet . . . I want you . . . badly . . .'

Her stomach twisted in fierce excitement and her breathing roughened. He meant it, her whole body knew he meant it. His skin was burning, his body tense with arousal. She recognised the symptoms because they matched her own. She wanted him, more than she had ever wanted anything in her life before, but she was dumb, she couldn't admit it, because last time she had been so naïve with her confession of love—she had poured it out to him wide-eyed, believing he felt exactly the same, only to have her illusions shattered on her wedding night.

Simeon had not been in love with her, he had kissed her because she had thrown herself at him and once he had started making love to her he had got carried away, only to find himself trapped into a marriage he hadn't wanted. He had blamed her for that, and he had been violently angry, although she hadn't suspected that until they were married and alone in that bedroom, and then his rage had broken out, horrifying her.

She could never forget the shock of discovering that behind the cool mask he had worn until their wedding night itself, he had bitterly resented having to marry her. She should have known, of course; only a silly, blind schoolgirl would have dreamt that a man like Simeon Gerard might want to marry her—let alone believed that they could actually be happy together! Well, she had grown up, acquired a little more sophistication, and she knew a lot more about life now.

Simeon had very good reasons for wanting her to lose her head over him, and he could be very devious. How much of his passion was real? How much a charade, a mimicry of desire, intended just to get her into bed, and make sure she had his child?

She stiffened, her blue eyes opening wide, staring at the ceiling as if she saw pictures there, a film of that long-ago night, of her humiliation and misery.

That time, she had made a fool of herself—well, Simeon wasn't going to do it again.

She put both hands on his shoulders and shoved Simeon away, at the same time rolling sideways, off the bed, landing somehow on her feet.

Her sudden escape had taken Simeon completely by surprise. By the time he realised what was happening Juliet was running out of the door. She got to her own bedroom before he caught up with her although she heard him coming at a furious run. She slammed home the bolt and leaned on the door, breathing raggedly, tears in her eyes.

'Juliet!'

His voice was hoarse, and made her jump away, half afraid that he could reach her, touch her, even through a bolted door. Then she stopped and stared at the door panels, running the back of her hand over her wet eyes. She was safe in here. She was safe so long as he couldn't get too close to her. Away from those seductive hands which made her brain stop working, she could actually think. Hadn't she cried enough over him eight years ago?'

He snarled her name again. 'Juliet!'

'Don't shout at me!' she muttered, backing towards her own bed and sinking down on it.

There was a silence, then his voice changed; she could almost hear him thinking, that twisted mind of his working out a new strategy to deal with this changed situation.

'Why did you suddenly run away, Juliet? Did I frighten you? I didn't mean to—I went a little crazy.' His voice went husky, intimate with laughter. 'Your fault again.'

Oh, of course, it would be, she thought, her mouth tight.

'Every time I touch you, you go to my head,' he said, and she bit down on her lower lip.

She refused to be taken in by his flattery, but she couldn't help reacting to it, even though she knew he was surely lying. He had only been acting just now, when he had breathed like that, kissed her with such passion, but he had fooled her while she was in his arms, and if she wasn't careful he would fool her again, because she was vulnerable to him, and he knew it.

'I'm sorry if I frightened you,' he said in a gentle voice which might have fooled her if she hadn't remembered how he had deceived her in the past. 'I suppose I was expecting you to be more experienced than you are.' Another pause, then, still gently, 'You aren't, though, are you? Experienced, I mean. There must have been men, though. You're far too attractive to have spent the last eight years in a city like London without meeting any men. But if you did, they didn't get very far with you, did they?'

He sounded infuriatingly complacent, even smug, and her teeth met. She wanted to lie, tell him he was quite wrong, she had had a string of lovers, but that might make him even more determined to get her into bed. Would inexperience be a wiser card to play? If she told him the truth, that there had been no other lover since their wedding night, what would be his reaction? She moved uneasily and caught sight of her reflection in the dressing-table mirror. Her face was pale now, her blue eyes haunted, unsure.

The trouble was that in spite of everything she knew about him there was this ceaseless drag of attraction, this feeling flowing through her every time she heard his voice, saw him. She had to kill that emotion. But how?

'This Adam, for instance,' Simeon said, his voice toughening, 'tell me the truth about him—is he your lover?'

She bit her lip. Should she say yes? No, best to say nothing. Silence was her only defence. Let him think what he liked.

Simeon waited, then bit out, 'Whether he is or not, you aren't seeing him again, Juliet.'

She couldn't stay silent, then. Her anger made her snap back, 'I've told you once already—I'm a grown woman, not a child, and I'm not your possession. You aren't giving me orders or telling me who I can see and who I can't.'

His voice changed, grew coaxing. 'At least you're talking to me now— Juliet, open the door, we can't shout at each other through it! If you're so adult, start acting like one!'

'And give you the chance to get at me again?' she scornfully retorted. 'Not on your life. I feel safer with a door between us!'

She picked up the vibrations of his temper, even through the door. She couldn't be sure, but she thought he was grinding his teeth. After a moment, he said tersely, 'Just so long as you understand that you can't see your boyfriend again. I'm deadly serious about that, Juliet. You must see why. I'm not running the risk of losing Chantries because of some question mark hanging over our child. There are to be no other men in the picture until after the birth.'

'I'm not even listening to this!' she muttered furiously.

Simeon went on as calmly as if she hadn't said a thing, 'And to make sure of that, you'll come back to Chantries with me as soon as this snow thaws.'

'I'll do nothing of the kind!'

'You must live with me until the child is born,' he said in a patient voice, as though that was obvious.

'No!' She was getting desperate now; he was so obstinate in refusing to take her seriously.

'You don't have to be afraid, Juliet,' he murmured in that deceptively gentle voice. 'I won't force you. We have plenty of time to get used to each other again.'

He hadn't been gentle on their wedding night. Why should he be any different this time?

'Juliet!' he said sharply, after a while. 'Are you listening to me? Juliet, we can't talk like this. I want to see your face—open the door, I promise I won't even touch you.'

'Go away!' she muttered. 'You must be crazy, even suggesting it. You may be cold-blooded, but I'm not. I'm not sleeping with you, I couldn't stand having you touch me—and I'm certainly not having your child. I'm not going back with you, either. For one thing, I like my job, and I'm not giving it up, and for another, I never want to see Chantries again, so just go away, and leave me alone.'

She was so angry her voice was raw with it, and she picked up a book lying on her bedside table and threw it at the door. The violent gesture was some relief to her; she sagged afterwards, breathing thickly.

'You're overwrought,' Simeon said.

She shouted back at him, 'Don't you patronise me! I'm angry, that's what I am! And I have good cause!'

'Lie down and have a rest,' he merely said in a soothing voice which made her even more furious. 'We'll talk again later, when you're calmer.'

'I won't change my mind—I've nothing else to say,' she snapped, and this time he didn't bother to reply. She heard him walk back down the stairs and into the sitting-room, closing the door quietly.

Juliet threw herself full-length on to the bed and stared at the ceiling, trying to think clearly, but all that happened was that she drifted into a waking daydream about Simeon. She kept getting images of him: smiling at her, mocking her, kissing, caressing her. She tried to force her stupid imagination to remember other moments—Simeon looking at her with icy hostility, Simeon snarling at her, threatening her. It was useless. She remembered only what she secretly wanted to remember; her body was trembling with sensuality, and she despised herself for being so weak. It wasn't as if he hadn't told her with brutal honesty just why he was here! He had announced his intentions last night and only a few hours later she had been in his arms, ready to let him do as he liked with her. What sort of idiot was she?

She winced, closing her eyes. Don't answer that! she told herself. Think about something else. Work, think about work. How long will it be before the roads are clear enough to get back to London? She began devising ways and means of getting out of this cottage, getting back to London. Instead of counting sheep, she counted ways and means of escape, and began to yawn. She was very tired. It had been a disturbed and disturbing night, and she was mentally and physically exhausted. After a little while, she went to sleep, woke up as the room thickened with twilight.

Almost at once, Juliet remembered everything; she sat up with a little gasp and turned to look at the clock, taken aback to see that it was nearly seven o'clock in the evening.

She slid off the bed to look out at the moor. It seemed much lighter outside than it was in the house. The stars showed like the glittering points of swords in the midnight-blue sky. It was cold again, but the snow did not seem as deep. It had been as high as the garden wall, but now it had sunk and she could see plants showing through it. She peered out, frowning—was it her imagination, or was the snow melting?

She leant on the windowsill, staring out, for several minutes, but couldn't say for sure whether or not the thaw had begun. Maybe in the morning she would be able to drive back to London?

She seemed to have been here for days, so much had happened to her—yet it wasn't even twenty-

four hours since she had arrived. She would be glad
to get back, she told herself. She had to be glad.
It was the only sensible view to take.

She sighed and drew her curtains together, then
went over to switch on her bedroom light, before
walking into her bathroom to shower. She felt hot
and creased, for one thing, and for another she
needed to wash Simeon out of her hair.

The water cascaded down on her, deafening her
to all other sounds. When she had finished, she
turned off the overhead jet, and slid into her white
towelling robe, lightly towelled her hair and dried
her bare legs and feet before going back into her
bedroom.

She was padding across the carpet when she heard
the sound of a car engine.

Juliet stopped dead, her heart plunging sicken-
ingly. For a second she almost believed she was
imagining the noise, and then she knew she wasn't,
and ran to the window. Headlights cut through the
dusk and illumined the lane, showing her the large
black Land Rover slowly drawing up outside.

Who on earth could it be? she wondered, staring
at the vehicle as it parked beside the wall. A local
farmer, calling to enquire if she was OK? One of
her mother's friends who had noticed the lights?

Then the driver's door opened and someone
climbed out and turned to stare up at the cottage,
and Juliet drew a sharp breath, hardly believing her
eyes.

It was Adam.

# CHAPTER SIX

FOR a second Juliet was too stunned to think, and then her mind worked like crazy. Simeon was downstairs. He would open the door when Adam knocked, and she hated to think what might happen then! There was something aggressive in the set of Adam's shoulders as he began to walk towards the house. He and Simeon were going to clash, that was obvious, and she would love to watch Adam knock Simeon off his perch, but she somehow didn't feel optimistic. The most likely outcome of a fight between the two men was that Adam would get the worst of it, and since she was the reason for his being there it would be her fault if he got hurt, or humiliated any further, so she had to stop it happening.

She didn't stop to put on any clothes; there wasn't time. She just ran for the stairs and took them two at a time, but she was too late to stop Simeon opening the front door and eying Adam with disfavour.

'If you're looking for Mrs Mendelli, she isn't here.'

'I know that.' Adam was equally brusque. He was staring at Simeon coldly as Juliet reached them, and then his eyes moved to her and flicked up and down from her damp hair to her bare legs and feet, not missing the short white towelling robe which, more or less, covered the rest of her. His mouth hardened. 'So there you are, Juliet,' he said in a tone edged with ice.

Simeon gave her a sideways look, then did a double-take, his black brows meeting harshly.

'Go back upstairs and get dressed!' he snapped.

She glared back at him. 'Will you please go back into the sitting-room, and mind your own business? This is a friend of mine.'

'I've already guessed who he is,' Simeon drawled, giving Adam a brief, disparaging glance. 'And you aren't talking to him while you're half naked, so go and get some clothes on!'

'Stop giving her orders!' Adam intervened, scowling, and taking a step forward with the obvious intention of using his wide shoulders to barge Simeon out of his way.

Simeon laughed and Juliet's nerves leapt at the sound of that laughter, because she knew what was going to happen, and it did. Simeon's whole weight met Adam as he tried to push past into the cottage, and Adam was thrown backwards.

'No! Don't...' Juliet broke out tensely, then sighed with relief as she watched Adam land, not on the stone path, but more comfortably in a thick laurel bush which cushioned his fall.

Simeon began to shut the door on him, but Juliet grabbed the handle too, struggling with him, her flushed face turned up towards his in an angry stare.

'Will you stop acting as though you own everything? You don't own this house and you don't own me—and you don't have any right to throw my friends out!'

Adam had got back on his feet. Very red and absolutely furious, he lurched back towards them both, snarling, 'You wait till I get you, you lunatic!'

'Oh, I'm scared,' mocked Simeon, his lean body poised for action, but Juliet moved swiftly in front of him and faced Adam, her eyes dark with apology.

'Adam, I'm so sorry about that, but you shouldn't have tried to force your way past him. He has a filthy temper.'

'I have nothing of the kind!' Simeon denied, his hands closing on her waist as he tried to lift her out of the way.

She slapped his hands down. 'Don't manhandle me, Simeon! Go away.' She gave Adam a pleading look. 'Adam, you shouldn't have come down here—what on earth made you do it?'

'Who's he?' Adam grated, staring past her at Simeon. 'That's what I came here to find out. Who is he? It was him on the phone this morning, wasn't it? What did he mean, he was your husband? He isn't your husband, is he, Julie?'

'Yes,' Simeon said.

At the same time Juliet said, 'No!' then Simeon laughed and she gave a cross little sigh and said, 'Well, yes and no, actually, Adam. It is a long story, and this isn't the time to explain.'

'Oh, I've got all night,' he said in a clipped voice. 'I'm certainly not driving back to London until I know the whole truth, and, anyway, I'm tired— I'm not doing that return journey until tomorrow, and it is far too late to get a hotel room somewhere, even if I knew a hotel, so I'd be grateful if you would let me stay here tonight. Anything would do—a couch, if there's nothing else.'

'Not on your life!' Simeon said, but Juliet had had time to think and she realised that Adam's arrival was the miracle she had been praying for, so she eagerly nodded.

'Of course you can stay, Adam.'

'No! Let him go to a hotel,' said Simeon.

'Will you stay out of this?' Juliet smiled at Adam. 'We can do better than a couch—there's a very comfortable bedroom free.'

'Thank you,' he said rather stiffly. 'I've got an overnight bag in my car, but I'll get it later.' Something in his expression told her that he was afraid that if he went back to his car now he might find the front door locked against him on his return.

Nodding, she stepped back and waved him into the sitting-room. 'Come in here, it's much warmer. Do sit down.' She was nervously talking politely, as though to an acquaintance who had called socially. 'Can I get you anything? You must be frozen, after that long drive. Would you like a hot drink? Coffee? Tea?'

Adam stayed on his feet, facing her, his expression belligerent. He was clearly in no mood to make polite conversation. All he replied was: 'First, I'd just like the truth, however long it takes. Is that guy your husband, or isn't he?'

Simeon lounged in the doorway, listening to them both, and she was very aware that he was there although she didn't look that way.

'Well, yes, in a way,' she huskily said, and Adam's face tightened. Hurriedly, she went on,

'Adam, I was seventeen, we were married for one day, then I left, and I haven't seen him since, until he turned up down here. That's why I said we weren't really married, and, believe me, we'll be getting a divorce.'

'No,' said Simeon coolly. 'We won't.'

'Take no notice of him,' Juliet crossly said. 'I should have started divorce proceedings years ago, but I didn't want to marry again, and I was reluctant to get in touch with him to make arrangements, even through a solicitor, so I kept putting it off.'

Adam's brow was furrowed. 'I don't understand this—you got married and left the same day? Why? What happened?' He shot Simeon a hostile look. 'What did he do to you?'

She was tempted to tell him, but decided it would only lead to another fight between the two men, so she just said shortly, 'It didn't work out.'

Adam's jaw dropped. 'Didn't work out?'

Simeon answered him because Juliet had gone pink, realising how that had sounded, and was temporarily lost for words.

'No, she didn't give it much of a chance, did she?' he drawled, his face ironic. 'She panicked on our wedding night and ran out on me. My fault, I suppose; I should have realised she was by no means as adult as she seemed, but she had done quite a job of covering up before the wedding. She acted like a woman until the time came to prove she was one, and then she chickened out.

'I was only seventeen!' she muttered rather resentfully. 'If I acted like a woman around you until we were married it was because I was trying out the role. That's what we do, isn't it? Whether we're men or women, we practise being adult long before we actually are...'

'Well, you had me fooled,' he drily said, and she looked down, biting her lip, knowing there was nothing she could say to that.

'You might have told me,' Adam said, his face sullen. 'You knew I was thinking of marrying you. You should have told me you weren't free—it was very unfair of you to date me all this time without making your situation clear.'

'I'm sorry, Adam,' she said, looking at him regretfully. 'You're right—of course I should have told you, but, you see, it never entered my head because I'd almost forgotten I was married.'

'But you are,' Simeon bit out, his eyes threatening. 'And you're staying married, so you can forget any idea of divorce.'

'Take no notice of him!' Adam said scathingly. 'He can't stop you getting a divorce, and he knows it. A marriage that only lasted one day? And then eight years' separation? It's a foregone conclusion. That adds up to irretrievable breakdown of the marriage; you couldn't have better grounds for divorce. As soon as we're back in London you can contact your lawyers and start the proceedings, and there'll be nothing he can do about it.'

'And how will you live with yourself afterwards?' Simeon conversationally asked her, his face cool. 'When my cousin and his family take over Chantries?'

She stared back at him, biting her lip, her face uncertain and disturbed.

'What?' Adam asked, looking from one to the other of them. 'What's he talking about now?'

'None of your business,' Simeon said. 'Why don't you go and get your bag from your car and take yourself off upstairs?'

Juliet pulled herself together and gave Adam a pleading little smile. 'Yes, maybe you should do that. You could probably do with a bath, you must be frozen and that will make you feel much better. I'm afraid you'll have to have a scratch supper, we don't have much fresh food and we're living mainly out of tins, but I'll do my best. It should be ready in an hour or so.'

He hesitated. 'If I go out to the car, will he try to lock me out, though?'

'No,' she promised. 'I'll make sure he won't, don't worry.'

Adam shrugged, nodded, and walked out, and Simeon gave Juliet a cool look which moved over her from head to foot, making her very conscious of her nakedness under the short open-lapelled robe.

'Go upstairs and get dressed, will you? It's very distracting having you standing around in almost nothing at all, and I don't like the way he was staring, either.'

She held her lapels together with one hand, giving him a resentful stare back.

'I'll go once Adam is back. I'm not having you lock him out.'

'He's just as you described him,' Simeon observed conversationally. 'Boring, conventional, small-minded. What on earth did you ever see in him?'

She ignored him, watching the door for signs of Adam's return while Simeon watched her like a cat at a mousehole, but this cat could wait all night, she thought, it wasn't going to get what it was waiting for. She knew he was trying to taunt her into a flare of rage, and she knew why. He didn't want her staying calm and collected, in control of herself. Well, she did—and she had every intention of staying calm until she could get away from him.

'Surely he wasn't the best you could find?' drawled Simeon.

She ignored him, but she wished he would stop assessing her with those flicking grey eyes, lingering on the long, smooth bare legs visible below the hem of her robe, the way the damp towelling clung to her hips and the indentation above her thighs, or the deep V-neck where her lapels met. She was still holding her lapels there, trying to hide the glimpse of her breasts he might get, but his eyes kept coming back upwards, making her feel uneasily that he could see far more than she wanted him to see.

'He isn't in love with you, you know. He's possessive, maybe, and he may see you as one of his possessions, but he hasn't lost his head over you. It doesn't go very deep with him.' His brows curved sardonically. 'I would even doubt if anything did.'

She still didn't give any sign of having heard him, but she was very relieved to hear Adam coming back, closing the door behind him. She walked out to meet him in the hall, smiled at him placatingly.

'I'll show you to your room.'

'I'll do that,' Simeon said behind her.

'This is not your house—you're as much a guest as he is!' she snapped, suddenly at the end of her tether. 'It's my mother's house, and I'm going upstairs anyway, so I'll show him.'

Adam didn't smile but he had a certain smugness as he followed her up the stairs, and, contrarily, that irritated her because she knew he had been delighted to hear her put Simeon in his place, and Adam had no right to smirk about that.

But she didn't want to quarrel with Adam, because his arrival had probably saved her from making a disastrous mistake. If he hadn't come when he did she might have ended up in bed with Simeon and her whole life could have been blighted. If she had become pregnant, she would have had to spend the next nine months at Chantries, waiting for his child to be born, and then, of course, he would want to keep the baby there with him, which would have left her with a terrible decision to face. Should she stay with her baby, and Simeon, knowing that he only wanted her as the mother of the child—or desert her baby and divorce its father? Whatever she decided there would be grief and pain ahead for her, and she had had enough of that eight years ago when she ran away from him and their brief marriage. She was very grateful to Adam for coming all this way.

Opening the door of the third bedroom, which was the smallest of the three, Juliet gave Adam an apologetic look. 'It isn't very spacious, I'm afraid, but it is warm and comfortable, I think.'

He looked around the little box-room, his mouth wry. The furniture was all made of golden pine: just a single bed, with a box cabinet next to it on which stood a glass table lamp, a small chest of drawers, a narrow wardrobe. The curtains and carpet were a spring-like green, the walls painted glossy white.

'It's very pretty,' Adam politely said, although they both knew that it wasn't what he was used to and that he did not like this rural style of furnishing. Adam was an urban man; he liked well-cut suits, elegant décor in his home, French restaurants and city streets. There was nothing for him in this bleak, moorland setting.

'I'm sorry you had this long journey for nothing,' Juliet said, and he shrugged.

'So am I. God knows why I came. I should have my head examined, but that phone call worried me. I couldn't believe you were married, but that fellow had cut me off, and when I rang back he did the same thing again, and I began to think maybe something was seriously wrong here, that he was some madman who had got hold of you and...' He broke off, grimacing, his face darkly flushed. 'Oh, well, you know. I started imagining what could be happening to you, and...'

He stopped again, swallowing and looking sheepish, and Juliet was suddenly touched, and smiled at him.

'That was nice of you, Adam, coming to rescue me!' Then her blue eyes widened and she gave a gasp. 'Adam! It's tonight, isn't it? You're going to miss it!'

He inclined his head without saying anything, and she stared at him, quite speechless for a second. It was a sacrifice she would never have expected him to make, and it amazed and moved her.

'Oh, Adam ... and I'd forgotten all about it, I'm so sorry.' She bit her lower lip guiltily, realising she should have thought of it at once when she first saw him. He had talked of nothing else but the firm's ball for weeks. 'I know how much it meant to you to be there!' she murmured apologetically. 'Adam, you shouldn't have given it up for me, you really shouldn't! It was wonderful of you to be so worried about me, and I am very grateful, but you should just have rung the police and asked them to check that I was OK.'

He gave her an odd look, hesitated, then said rather offhandedly, 'Well, I did ring them, actually, but it took me ages to get anyone to talk to me— first of all they just said I should leave a message. Their operator said they were very busy, because of the snow; there had been lots of road accidents. I insisted on talking to someone, and a sergeant came on the line, but he didn't seem to be taking me very seriously. I explained that you were here alone, but that when I rang up some man answered the phone and was very aggressive with me, said he was your husband, which I knew couldn't be true...' Adam was very flushed, his eyes furious. 'But this policeman seemed to find it rather amusing. He didn't laugh, but he sounded as if he might be grinning. He said you could have lied to me, been married all the time. He said it sounded like a domestic matter, and they didn't interfere in domestic matters. I could tell he wasn't going to do anything about it, so in the end I decided I had to come myself.'

'That was very kind and thoughtful of you,' she soothed, quite moved by the realisation that he had thrown away the chance to impress his bosses at the firm's annual celebration, just to come and rescue her from what he had imagined might be terrible danger.

Adam gave her a sideways look, scowled, and burst out resentfully, 'Yes, and now I find the police were quite right, all along—you were lying to me, you are married, and I've been a fool.'

'It isn't like that,' she burst out, going pale. 'I didn't lie...at least, not deliberately. I had forgotten I was married——'

'How could you forget a thing like that?' he demanded in a biting voice, his face hostile.

'It was so long ago, and I was so young, and it didn't seem real, any of it. It was like a dream I had had, and escaped from. I didn't tell you because it simply didn't occur to me, not because I was trying to pull the wool over your eyes.'

Adam fell silent, his face brooding, then said grimly, 'Even if that's all true, I'm surprised your mother, at least, didn't say anything. I'd made it clear I was planning to marry you—she might have warned me——'

'She didn't know! I never told her. I never told anybody. I just wanted to forget all about Simeon, the wedding, everything. I blotted it out—I suppose I wished it had never happened.'

'I'm not surprised,' Adam said, his jawline belligerent. 'That guy is a nasty piece of work, if ever I've seen one. What was he threatening you with just now? Something about a chantry, and you being sorry if you divorced him? What did he mean?'

She hesitated, looking down, her dark lashes lying on her pale cheek. She couldn't face telling Adam about Robert Gerard's will, or the demand Simeon had made in consequence.

'Chantries is his family home,' she said vaguely. 'He wants me to go back there with him.'

'Oh,' Adam said, frowning. 'I see. Family home? Does that mean the fellow's rich?'

'His family are very wealthy,' she admitted. 'They've owned the estate for generations, and there is a lot of land attached to the house.'

Adam grunted dissatisfaction. 'That explains a lot. Born with a silver spoon in his mouth, was he? Arrogant swine. I can't stand men of his kind.'

She was tempted to smile, but somehow managed to keep a straight face, knowing that Adam disliked men who were born into wealth and power, and yet dreamt of one day acquiring all the things they inherited by birthright. His dislike of men like Simeon was not ideological, it was simple jealousy; he wanted what they had.

Gently, she said, 'Well, thank you, anyway, Adam, for coming to my rescue. You're looking very tired. Why don't you lie down and rest for an hour while I go and get dressed, then cook supper?'

She slipped out of the room, closing the door behind her, and went into her own bedroom, only to stop short on finding Simeon waiting there for her. He was lying full-length on her bed, his hands behind his head, his lean body totally relaxed, and her pulses began to go crazy at the sight of him, which made her even angrier at finding him there.

'What do you think you're doing in here?' she spat at him, keeping her voice down so that Adam shouldn't hear them. She did not want another scene between the two men.

'Isn't it obvious?' drawled Simeon. 'I've been waiting for you to come out of his room. What took you so long?' His tone was light but his eyes were deadly and she was not fooled by the smile curling his mouth. Simeon was at his most dangerous when he looked this casual and laid-back.

'We were talking,' she said curtly. 'Look, I want to get dressed. Will you get out of here and give me a little privacy? If you want to talk to me, you can do it downstairs.'

He stayed where he was, still smiling with his mouth while his grey eyes were dagger sharp. 'Talking? All this time?' He lifted an arm, glanced down at his watch, his black brows lifting. 'You must have had a lot to say to each other. Why did you have to say it in his bedroom? Why not downstairs, where I could hear you?'

'That's why not!' she bit out, her blue eyes icy. 'We didn't want you standing there, listening to every word, and interrupting whenever you felt like it! Can't you get it through your head that I have a life of my own, and you don't control it?'

He gestured that aside arrogantly, his face hard. 'Well, from now on, you don't go into any bedrooms alone with him, is that clear?'

'From now on, you don't walk into my bedroom, is *that* clear?' she furiously threw back. 'And stop giving me orders. Get off my bed and go away so that I can get dressed!'

'I've seen you naked before,' he said, a glitter of cold mockery in his grey eyes, and watched, smiling, as hot colour ran up her face.

'Get out!' she snapped.

He swung his long legs off the bed and stood up, and she backed, nervous of him even now that Adam was within earshot if she did need to scream for help.

Simeon began to saunter towards the door, then twisted sideways without warning and caught hold of her, his hands closing on her arms, pulling her ruthlessly towards him until their bodies touched.

She began to tremble at the intimate contact, but her head went back and her chin lifted defiantly. 'Let go or I'll call Adam!' she threatened.

He laughed under his breath. 'And what do you think he could do?'

'He——' she began angrily, only to have her voice stifled by his mouth coming down against her lips. She tried to go on talking, but the movement of her mouth merely gave him the chance to deepen the kiss, and she moaned in a sort of anguish, torn between pleasure and rage. He had discovered her vulnerability to him and he didn't scruple to take advantage of it, but she knew his emotions weren't involved, so why was she allowing him to do this to her? He was using his head, not following his heart, and if she let him seduce her into going back with him to Chantries, living with him again as his wife, in every sense of the word, she would be insane.

He stopped kissing her and smiled down at her flushed, confused, uncertain face. 'You're lovelier now than you were at seventeen, you know. Oh, you were sexy then—you were a very precocious adolescent and I wanted you badly, but you were too skinny and wide-eyed to be really sexy. Your figure has improved beyond recognition, you know how to dress and wear make-up, and you're far more sure of yourself, more sophisticated. I think a woman needs the glitter of sophistication to make her really sexy, don't you?'

'I . . .' she began, stammering because the way he was looking at her made her shudder, made her throat beat with a hunger which terrified her. Did he really find her sexy? Or was he just telling her that to trap her?

He brushed his mouth down her throat, murmuring huskily against her skin, 'I want you far more now than I ever did eight years ago.'

Her heart missed a beat. He's lying, she thought desperately. He must be lying. But common sense couldn't stop her body from reacting violently to what he was doing to it, his hands slipping intimately inside her robe, softly caressing her neck, her shoulders, her naked breasts.

She wanted to push him away, but she couldn't, because she loved it, she ached for the touch of his hands, and she wanted him with an intensity she hadn't even suspected she could feel eight years ago. The teenager who had had such a crush on him simply hadn't had a clue about love.

'We made a bad beginning, Juliet,' Simeon said, looking down at her with a darkly brooding face. 'We made a mess of it all, both of us. I know I was a swine to you that night, and I've bitterly regretted it since, but we have a chance to start again, don't you see? Don't throw it away.'

She stared at him, silenced, her face pale and uncertain, and after a moment he let go of her and stepped back. 'I'll go down and start work on our supper, shall I?'

Huskily, she said, 'Thank you.'

He was gone a second later, and she bolted her door after him, then stood there, her mind in a state of total confusion. How much of all that had he meant? She no longer knew what to believe—he was driving her crazy, and she didn't know how much more of his bewildering, disturbing behaviour she could stand. Thank heavens the snow had begun to thaw and in the morning she would probably be able to drive back to London. Even if the roads were still icy, she could leave her car here at the cottage, in the locked garage and go back with Adam in his Land Rover, which could handle bad road conditions rather better than her own car. One way or another, though, she was determined to get away from Simeon and back to the hectic bustle of the city, which would seem so restful after the so-called calm and tranquillity of the countryside, if Simeon was there.

She pulled herself together; there wasn't time to think about this, she had to get dressed. She did so without really thinking much about what she was putting on, brushed her hair, put on a little light make-up, and went downstairs to help him with the supper.

He was stirring something in a saucepan, and turned to eye her speculatively from head to foot. 'Very neat,' he mocked. 'I'm quite sure the boy-friend will approve.'

She caught sight of herself reflected in the little mirror on the kitchen wall and knew what he meant, although she refused to admit it to him. She had automatically put on a black skirt, a demure white blouse and a warm black V-necked pullover, returning to the safety of city formality.

'Did I say you were sexy? I take it back,' Simeon said, turning down the heat under the pan of vegetable soup he had ready. 'Very tame tonight, aren't we? For his sake?' His grey eyes taunted. 'Or mine? Are you making sure I don't find you quite so sexy while he's around?'

Unconsciously, she might well have been, but she just shrugged, trying to look impatient. 'I simply put on the first thing that came to hand. You're reading too much into it.' She lifted another saucepan lid; he was boiling water. 'What is this for?' she asked.

'Rice,' he said. 'I've found some more tinned tomatoes, a tin of mixed beans, and a tin of tuna...that should make a reasonable meal for three, with this soup to start with, although that only comes out of a packet, I'm afraid, but it smells good and it will help fill us.'

'I'm starving,' she confessed. 'This seems to have been a very long day, and I'm mentally exhausted.'

Simeon put a friendly arm around her and smiled into her eyes. 'You slept all afternoon, and you're still tired?'

'So much has happened since I woke up,' she complained, leaning on him and feeling her body slacken and give itself up to his support.

'It has been an eventful day,' he agreed, then his glance skated over her head towards the kitchen door and his face iced over. 'Oh, there you are— supper is nearly ready,' he said coldly, and Juliet stiffened and looked round, too, moving out of the circle of his arm.

Adam came right into the room, scowling. 'Sorry to interrupt!'

'You aren't interrupting,' Juliet hurriedly said. 'Simeon has cooked us a terrific pot luck meal, so let's eat now, shall we?'

The meal was not exactly *cordon bleu*, but it was very warming and filling, and Juliet would have eaten it even if it hadn't been, because she was very hungry. They all washed up together, making stiff polite small talk about the weather. Outside the melting snow dripped from the roof, from trees, and water ran somewhere in a gutter, or down a path. It was much warmer, too. They drank their coffee in the sitting-room, still trying to be polite, then listened to a play on the radio for an hour.

When the play ended, they listened to a news bulletin, with the two men commenting on some international news on which they, naturally, disagreed violently. They had nothing in common, especially not their opinions, and Juliet was weary of their sniping at each other, so she got up, said goodnight and left them to fight without their audience.

She fell asleep almost as soon as her head hit the pillow, and woke in a pale, cloudy light which turned out to be morning. Looking at her watch, she found it was half-past seven, so she got up. When she was washed and dressed, she looked out of her window and saw that the snow was almost gone—the road still had a few icy patches, but she was certain she could safely set out for London.

She packed and went down to find Adam already up, drinking coffee and eating some rather dusty-looking cornflakes.

'This was all I could find,' he gloomily said.

'That's OK. We can stop on the road,' she said. 'I've decided to leave my car here and go back in yours—is that OK?'

He put down his spoon and stared at her. 'Fine—have you told what's his name?'

She shook her head. 'I'd rather leave before he gets up, if you don't mind.'

'Running away?' Adam said drily, but he didn't ask her any more questions, just finished his coffee, offered her some, and, when she refused it, went off to get his overnight bag. Juliet quietly went out of the cottage and stared across the moorland which glimmered with opalescent mist, praying that Adam wouldn't wake Simeon.

Adam came out, carrying his packed bag, and she softly closed the door behind them, hearing it automatically lock. 'Should you leave him alone in the cottage?' Adam asked, frowning. 'Do you think that's wise?'

'He isn't a criminal,' Juliet said impatiently. 'When he leaves, the door will lock behind him, and he won't be able to get back in, anyway, so there's no problem.'

'Don't you think your mother would object, if she ever finds out, though? I mean, leaving a stranger alone in her cottage?'

'He isn't a stranger. She knows him, she's known him since he was a boy.'

Adam stopped in his track and stared at her. 'But you said she didn't know about the marriage.'

'She didn't, but she knows Simeon. I told you, my parents were divorced and I stayed with my father, who has always worked on Chantries, the Gerard estate—he still does, in fact, he's the head gamekeeper. My mother knew the Gerard family, including Simeon—but she left years before... before we were married.'

'I don't understand any of this,' Adam said, and she threw an anxious look back at the cottage, afraid she might see a curtain stir, a face appear. If Simeon saw them leaving, he would come after them, and urgency churned in her veins.

'Come on, Adam! There isn't time to argue. Let's get away while we can!'

Adam caught the nervousness in her voice, and walked hurriedly over to the Land Rover, unlocked it, and threw their luggage into the back, while

Juliet climbed up into the driver's cab. Adam slid behind the wheel and started the engine, then they began to move off. Juliet glanced anxiously into the wing mirror but there was no sign of movement in the cottage. Simeon must be sleeping like the dead.

Adam was driving carefully—the road conditions were still icy—but slowly the cottage vanished into the distance, and Juliet sank back, sighing with a shaky mixture of relief and painful regret. She couldn't have agreed to go back to him, but leaving hurt as much, if not more, than it had hurt her when she ran away from him after their wedding night.

'Is that it, then?' Adam asked suddenly. 'Are you going to divorce him, or not? I mean, it all seems very confused, a real muddle. Don't you think you'd better regularise it? Especially as you seem scared of the fellow.'

'I'm not scared of him!' she denied resentfully.

'It looks like it to me!' said Adam, and of course it did, she knew that, and it was true. She was scared of Simeon; wary of him, too, the way any sane person would be wary of a wild animal out of its cage and prowling around looking for prey.

'Obviously I shall divorce him,' she said in a flat tone, angry with herself because just saying that made her feel depressed. Their marriage had never been a real one; why should it upset her to think of ending it?

'But will he make difficulties?' Adam thought aloud, and again he had hit the nail right on the head.

That was just what Simeon would do—make difficulties. And he would start making them the minute he woke up in the cottage and discovered she had fled. He wasn't going to let her escape without making some sort of effort to get her back. He had too much to lose. He would come after her, and fast, and Juliet felt her nerves crackle like a forest fire at the very prospect of Simeon on her trail, stalking her remorselessly until he managed to corner her.

She looked at the speedometer, her blue eyes feverish. Adam was doing a calm and steady forty miles an hour, and no doubt that was wise, on these slippery roads, but panic had set in now and Juliet was desperate to get to London before Simeon caught up with them.

'Can't you go any faster?' she snapped, and Adam gave her a startled, sideways look. 'He'll be coming after us any minute now,' Juliet warned, and Adam's skin paled, he swallowed convulsively, abandoned caution and put his foot down on the accelerator.

## CHAPTER SEVEN

JULIET was asleep when Adam eventually pulled up outside her flat. He touched her arm, and she woke with a start, blinking sleepily up at him. For a few seconds her face was blank, then everything came back to her and she sat up, brushing her chestnut hair back from her flushed face.

'Where are we?'

'Your place,' Adam said in stiff, offended tones. It had not been an easy journey; for the first hour he had fired questions at her and disliked all her answers, and she had been too impatient and irritable to be diplomatic—she didn't see that he had any right to sit in judgement on either her or Simeon, and had said so, which, of course had led to a nasty little row. At last she had simply refused to speak to him at all, had closed her eyes, turning away, and gone to sleep.

'Already?' she said, with relief, looking out of the car at the familiar building, the quiet street. 'You made good time.' He must have driven like a maniac. A glance at her watch told her that it was only one o'clock, lunchtime—and immediately after that she began to feel hungry.

'There wasn't much traffic about.' Adam shrugged. 'The snow must have kept most people off the roads.' He got out and lifted down her luggage and Juliet joined him on the pavement, warily contemplating the curtained windows of her flat. Simeon couldn't have possibly have got here first; Adam had driven far too fast. No doubt he would be hard on their heels, though.

'Shall I come up with you, to make sure everything is OK?' Adam asked politely, apparently reading her expression, and she shook her head.

'No, I'll be fine. It is broad daylight, after all.' She picked up her suitcase. It wasn't heavy and she could manage it perfectly well. 'Thanks, Adam——' she began politely and he inclined his head, interrupting.

'Not at all. Goodbye, Juliet.'

He strode back to the Land Rover, slid behind the wheel, and a moment later was gone, leaving her on the pavement, staring after him. Adam had meant that farewell; finality had echoed in his voice.

He had threatened to end their relationship if she didn't go to the ball, yet he had driven all the way to Cornwall because he was worried about her, and she was grateful to him for that, and felt guilty, because it meant that Adam did care about her in his own way. Would she have done the same, in his place? She considered that wryly, then smiled. Yes, of course she would. She hadn't been in love with him, but she had liked him, she had cared enough to help him if she thought he was in trouble. He was a friend, and she was sorry that she was unlikely ever to see him again.

But she wasn't going to cry. It had been a lukewarm affair from the beginning and she was grateful to him for walking away without further recriminations. He could have been much nastier.

Adam's pride was hurt; so was his self-esteem. He had had her tagged as a suitable wife, and he had made a mistake about her; he felt she had made a fool of him. He had lost his chance to impress his bosses at the firm's ball, on her account, only to discover that she had been married all the time, and married to a man like Simeon Gerard, exactly the type Adam most envied and detested.

She looked over her shoulder, suddenly nervous. What was she doing standing around out here when Simeon might roar up at any minute? She hurried into her flat and bolted the front door behind her, then went round the rooms, refusing to admit that she was checking that she was alone there.

Reassured about that, she unpacked and put all her clothes into the washing machine. She needed to wash everything she had worn at the cottage—the shirt Simeon had unbuttoned, the jeans he had unzipped, the towelling robe his hand had parted to explore her body. All her clothes seemed to her to be covered by his fingermarks. She almost felt like throwing them all away, never wearing them again, but that would be crazy; it would be admitting something she wasn't ready to admit.

She started the machine a few moments later, then hunted through her freezer for something simple to cook for lunch, deciding on a fish pie, cod and prawns under a potato lid.

She had almost finished eating it when the phone rang. She jumped up, her nerves going haywire. Was it Simeon?

Maybe she shouldn't answer it? But she wasn't capable of ignoring that shrill, insistent sound, so at last she picked it up.

'Hello?' she almost whispered.

'Oh, you *are* back!' her mother's voice said, and Juliet sagged, her heart slowing.

'Yes. Where are you? Still in Italy?'

'Just about!' Shirley Mendelli cheerfully told her. 'If you hadn't answered this time, I would have booked the next flight over, though. I've been trying to get hold of you all morning. First I rang you at the cottage for ages without getting a reply and then I rang here, then the cottage again, and I was so worried I was going to fly home today, but Giorgio said maybe you were on your way back to London, and not to panic...'

Juliet smiled, imagining the scene, typical of both of them—her mother always did go to extremes and Giorgio always soothed her down, as calm as a millpond and taking the common-sense point of view.

'Then I realised that if you were driving back you would leave around breakfast time, so I waited a couple of hours before starting again and got you right away. I tell you, I'm very relieved to hear your voice! How was the drive back to London? Were the roads tricky?'

'No, we had no trouble. The thaw is well under way now, and there wasn't much traffic.'

'We?' repeated her mother curiously. 'Did Sim Gerard drive you back?'

Juliet hesitated, realising how much of what had happened that weekend she couldn't tell her mother. 'No, Adam did, actually.'

'Adam? You didn't say he had gone down there with you.'

'He didn't come with me, he drove down to bring me back to town, in a Land Rover he had borrowed from a friend...'

'Why a Land Rover?'

'Good in bad road conditions,' Juliet brusquely said.

'Oh, yes. Well, that was thoughtful of him. Darling, do you want me to come back at once? Giorgio has to stay here for a few more days, but I could come alone—if you need me?'

'No, Mum, don't be silly! There are no problems here. You stay with Giorgio; he needs you more than we do!' Juliet urged, hoping she sounded convincing. She didn't want her mother to suspect she had anything worrying her; there was nothing she could do to help, after all.

'Sure you can cope with everything at work?'

'Of course I can! I'm looking forward to being in charge!' Juliet said lightly, but in a way she meant it seriously—being fully occupied in dealing with the business would stop her brooding over Simeon.

Her mother laughed. 'Well, in that case—have fun, darling, and thank you. It's such a help to know you're there, looking after things. But if you need me, I'll fly back at once—you only have to ask, you know that.'

'I know,' Juliet said, knowing she wouldn't ask, couldn't ask. There was too much she had hidden, too much she had never told her mother, and when Shirley heard the whole story she was going to be hurt at being excluded. Would she understand why her daughter had never felt able to confide in her? Why she had only wanted to forget her marriage and what had led up to it? One day, soon, Juliet knew she was going to have to tell her—but not while she was so far away, with worries of her own to fret about.

Juliet was on tenterhooks for the rest of the day, waiting for Simeon to arrive, or ring, but there was no sign of him, and by ten o'clock she had stopped expecting him. That was when she went to bed, but not to sleep. She lay there wide awake for hours, her mind working in ever-decreasing circles.

Her mother had had no reply when she rang the cottage, so Simeon must have left there, and he must have done so early in the morning. Where was he? It was obvious, she decided; he must have driven back to Chantries, not come to London. Why had he done that, though? She had been so certain he would follow her.

Had he abandoned his plan? Had he given up because she had fled with Adam? She couldn't believe it. Simeon wasn't that easily beaten. He had too much at stake; he had put his whole life into Chantries and he wasn't going to lose it if he could do anything to stop it.

Even when she fell asleep she kept waking up. She would sit up in bed suddenly and look dazedly, wildly, about her, as if there was someone or something in the room with her. It was like being haunted. Each time she would realise she was alone, sigh heavily, lie down again and go back to sleep.

Her alarm woke her at seven-thirty and she felt like death as she staggered out of bed and went through her usual routine before setting off for work. She looked out of the window before she left her flat; there was no sign of Simeon's car or of him, so she hurried out and got into her own car.

Her secretary looked up quickly as she walked into the office. 'Oh, good morning. How did your weekend trip go?' Helen knew she had had to drive down to Cornwall. 'I saw that they had snow in the west—did you have any problems down there?'

'I was snowed in for a day, but it soon thawed,' Juliet said, picking up the pile of letters waiting for her on her desk and flipping through them. 'Any messages?' she casually asked, not looking at Helen. He wouldn't have rung here, though—or would he? It would be the last thing she would expect, and so he might have done it.

'I left two on your desk—the Italian suppliers, ringing up about the next delivery.' Helen paused, her brow furrowed, then said in a faintly anxious voice, 'Oh, by the way, somebody rang to ask for you on Friday evening, just as I was leaving. He said it was urgent that he speak with you, but I thought I'd better not give him the address or phone number of the cottage. I hope that was OK?'

Juliet gave her a grim smile. 'Yes, you were quite right. Never give that sort of personal information out without checking with me first.'

Helen nodded. 'Well, that's a relief. He got quite angry, and kept saying he was a relative of yours, and I wasn't sure I'd done the right thing.'

She was a thin quiet girl with luxuriant brown hair and dark eyes. Her smile, when it came, was gentle and sweet-natured, but she didn't smile, or talk, easily. Helen was shy. She was very capable, and worked hard, but it was difficult to get her to talk about herself.

Juliet knew very little about her life outside the office. She liked her, and trusted her implicitly, but she often wondered why Helen was so secretive. She knew better than to ask direct questions, though, and now she just smiled encouragingly at her secretary and said, 'Well, we'd better get on with some work, hadn't we? Where are those balance sheets I was working on on Friday?'

Helen produced them from the files she kept in such excellent order, and the usual busy silence settled down over the small office. Juliet had been promoted to having her own office and secretary a year ago, after having worked in the various shops, taken a business course, and then shared an office with her mother's secretary, so that she could understudy her mother's job before Shirley and Giorgio moved up to Manchester to open the new shop there.

There was an increasing amount of administration involved in running the various shops, and they all knew that more secretarial staff had to be taken on sooner or later, but Shirley and Giorgio had a deeply rooted instinct to keep the firm a family one. They were afraid of expanding too fast,

in spite of the advice constantly urged on them by
their accountants. She suspected that they thought
that if the company got too big it would get out of
control, or, at least, out of their control, and she
could sympathise with that. A strong part of the
fun of the job, for everyone who worked for them,
at all levels, was the very personal style of
management.

Since the workload had doubled over the past
couple of years, however, that had left Juliet with
a great deal to do, but although she had sometimes
complained about that she was glad of it that week
because it kept her too busy to think about Simeon.

She was very on edge as she worked in her office
or drove around the stores, constantly wondering
if and when Simeon was going to appear. He didn't,
which should have been a relief, but somehow
wasn't. She was sleeping badly, and the tension was
eating at her nerves.

Was that why he was doing it? Was he trying to
rattle her? If that was it, he was doing a great job.
Whatever she was doing, half her mind was on him.

If he knew that, he would be triumphant, she
thought angrily, handing a pile of letters she had
just signed back to Helen with a glare which made
the other girl look very worried.

'Did I make a mistake?'

'What?' Juliet pulled herself together and grimaced. 'No, they were perfectly typed. Thanks. Sorry,
Helen, I was thinking about something else.'

'Is anything wrong?' Helen uncertainly asked,
watching her. 'You seem very...edgy...'

It was as rare for her to make a personal remark as it was for her to offer a confidence, so Juliet looked at her in surprise, then smiled.

'It's a personal problem—I shouldn't have brought it into work with me! Sorry, take no notice, Helen.' It was a relief to know that Helen wouldn't ask any more questions. At once, she nodded gravely and went back to her desk with the letters to be posted.

That evening, Juliet's mother rang to say that she and Giorgio could fly home at last, and would be on a flight next morning. 'We should be in Manchester by the early evening. I'll ring you when we get back home, darling. We'll probably come down to London in a couple of days to see you, and catch up with everything you've been up to. I suppose it's the usual horrible weather back there? Any more snow? Brr . . . I wish we could stay here, actually. We've been sunbathing and swimming, and it is going to be hell leaving.'

Juliet laughed. 'I believe you! But the weather has warmed up quite a bit over the last day or so. The sun came out today, and spring looks as if it is happening at last. Manchester isn't the Italian Riviera, but I don't think you'll freeze to death.'

She felt more cheerful as she went to bed. With her mother and Giorgio safely home, her life could get back to normal and she might stop looking over her shoulder all the time, or tensing every time the phone rang. She might even stop thinking about Simeon every waking second of the day, and wondering why he hadn't come looking for her. If only she knew why he had given up, she might be able to forget the whole strange episode.

She had another troubled night, and only fell asleep towards dawn, so deeply that her alarm didn't wake her. Luckily, a neighbour's radio did, playing pop music at a level that made her sit up, yawning, quite disorientated and almost believing the radio was in the bedroom with her. Pulling herself together, she looked at her clock to check the time and realised with a groan that she must have slept through the alarm. She was going to be very late for work this morning.

She stumbled out of bed just as the pop music stopped and a news bulletin began. Juliet was on her way to the bathroom, already pulling her white silk nightdress over her head, when she heard a familiar name through the thin walls.

'Chantries...'

Juliet froze in her tracks, half thinking she had imagined it, but the newsreader continued, 'One of the oldest houses in England, which has been in the possession of the same family since the Middle Ages.'

Why on earth would a news programme carry an item about Chantries? Juliet thought, frowning.

Then the newsreader went on, 'The cause of the fire has not yet been determined.'

Juliet gave a cry of shock, her hand going to her mouth. Oh, no! Oh, my God, no! she thought wildly; he set fire to the house to stop his cousin inheriting it!

'In the blaze, Mr Simeon Gerard, whose father, the previous owner, died last month, was taken to

Granville Hospital suffering from burns after being trapped in a bedroom and overcome by smoke. There were no other casualties and . . .'

The voice broke off and a gabble of other voices and music came through the wall as her neighbour switched restlessly from channel to channel. Frantically, Juliet ran to her own radio and switched it on, her hands shaking as she searched for the right station, but it took her a while to find it, and by the time she did the newsreader was dealing with another story.

Juliet tried other channels, switched on her TV, but no other news bulletin gave the story.

At last she gave up and hurried to shower and get dressed, her mind whirling in fear and anxiety. How badly had he been burnt? It sounded serious. What had the newsreader said exactly? Taken to hospital, suffering from burns after being trapped in a bedroom and overcome by smoke? That could be dangerous, even if you didn't get burnt. People often died from inhaling smoke.

She had to get to him, as fast as she could. What if he was . . .? She couldn't even think the word. Simeon was tough; he was a survivor. He wouldn't die. He mustn't, because if he did she'd want to die too.

She closed her eyes, trembling, white-faced. She loved him. She had always loved him, as long as she could remember. She hadn't just had a crush on him, or lost her head over him. She had kept telling herself that that was all she had felt; a teenage infatuation. But it had been far more than that. She had loved him, the way a woman loved—

deeply, passionately. She had tried to kill her love after their disastrous wedding night, she had tried to hate him, but love like that was not so easy to kill. The minute she had seen him again, it had flared up as fiercely and hungrily as before. She loved him so much that at times she had almost hated him, had felt like killing him.

Her blue eyes opened, enormous, their black pupils dilated and glittering like dark stars in her white face. Simeon loved Chantries like that, she thought, with a pang of fear. A line of poetry came into her head. 'Each man kills the thing he loves.'

She flinched. Oh, but Simeon couldn't have set fire to Chantries. He wouldn't do that. He loved the house too much, it meant too much to him. The idea was crazy; why on earth had she ever let herself think such a thing?

Simeon could be obsessive, he could be as unpredictable as a hurricane blowing out of nowhere, a possessive man whose emotions ran deep below the cool surface he showed everyone else, but he was also a very strong man, a man of integrity and honour. Why else had he felt bound to marry her although he had never intended to in the beginnng?

No, Simeon would never do anything to harm Chantries, even if he was going to lose it.

She rang Granville Hospital once she was sure her voice was steady, and was put through to the ward to which Simeon had been taken. The ward sister spoke to her politely. 'Are you a relative?'

Juliet hesitated, then said for the first time, 'I'm his wife.'

'Oh, yes, Mrs Gerard,' said the sister warmly. 'I have you down as his next of kin. He said you were away on holiday, touring, or we would have rung you to tell you. I hope it wasn't too much of a shock to hear the news. Did the police find you? He told them not to bother, but I expect they felt they should. He's quite comfortable. When do you think you'll get here?'

'Some time today, I can't say for sure exactly when,' Juliet said huskily. 'Sister, what does "quite comfortable" mean exactly? How serious are his injuries?'

'Don't worry, we're keeping him under permanent observation—shock can be a problem in these cases, and inhaling smoke can have after-affects which don't show up at once, but I think I can promise you that there is no need to be seriously worried.'

Juliet saw that she wasn't going to get a clear, factual answer; the ward sister was being far too carefully diplomatic. She would have to wait to know for sure how Simeon was when she could see for herself.

She rang Helen next, and warned her that she wouldn't be in to work. 'A friend has been in an accident, I'm going to see him in hospital, and it will take all day. Hold the fort, would you? Cancel any appointments, make new ones, and if any problems come up try to sit on them until I ring you later. My mother should be back this evening, thank heavens. I'll talk to her and, if necessary, ask if she can get to London tomorrow to take over for me.'

Helen was politely incurious. 'I see. I'll do my best—don't worry. Is there a phone number where I could reach you today?'

'Not yet,' Juliet said. 'I'll ring back later when I've got an address and phone number to give you.'

'Right,' Helen said, then quietly added, 'I hope your friend isn't too badly hurt, Juliet. I'll keep my fingers crossed for you.'

'Thanks,' Juliet said, and rang off.

Before she set off, she made a final phone call—to her mother's Manchester home. Of course there was nobody there, but she left a message on the answering machine, explaining what had happened and saying that she would ring with more news when she had any. Her mother would be puzzled by her dash to the hospital to see a man she had never mentioned once during the past eight years until last weekend, but Juliet had no time to explain yet. That was something she must face soon, and it was going to come as a terrible shock to Shirley Mendelli, but for the moment the only thing Juliet could think about was getting to Simeon.

## CHAPTER EIGHT

THE hospital stood among green lawns and formal circles of rosebeds on the outskirts of a small town some five miles from Chantries. It served not only the town, but the surrounding countryside, and Juliet could remember coming there when she had been just five years old to have her tonsils taken out. It had seemed vast to her, then, a towering threat of a building which had terrified her. That morning, as she walked towards it from the car park where she had left her car, the hospital seemed to have shrunk, yet she still felt a pang of fear, a nervous tremor, looking up at the place. She was afraid for Simeon; what if he was badly hurt? He was such an active man, with lots of energy—how was he going to bear to lie in bed for any length of time?

With the eyes of an adult she saw that the hospital was a ramshackle collection of buildings, of various periods and styles, which had been added on to a central Victorian house which had obviously been the original hospital, and which did have a certain solid style, almost a smugness about the way it stood there, with its rows of flat, unrevealing windows. Perhaps she should have found that complacency reassuring, but she didn't; it worried her, made her feel she was approaching a hostile place where nobody cared if you lived or died.

She walked under the massive portico, between the two huge stone pillars supporting the canopy, through the open double doors into a large hall full of wooden benches on which were seated out-patients waiting to see the casualty officer. She stood there, hesitating, feeling very out of place. Nobody looked round at her; the faces had a glazed patience, a lack of expectation of ever being seen by a doctor, which was vaguely depressing.

Juliet crossed to the porter in his little office and asked for directions, then set out to find the ward where Simeon had spent the night. It was a long walk; the corridors, with their smell of disinfectant and floor polish, seemed endless, but at last she pushed open the swinging door and saw a sister sitting a desk in a glass-walled little office.

'You want to see Mr Gerard?' The other woman gave her a quick, sharp look, then smiled sooth-ingly. 'Are you Mrs Gerard?'

Flushing slightly, Juliet nodded, and the sister said, 'Well, it isn't visiting hours but under the cir-cumstances...he's in the side-ward at the very end. Please, don't stay too long, it's nearly lunchtime.'

Under the circumstances? Juliet thought, her heart squeezed in the grip of fear as she walked through the busy ward. What had the woman meant by that? What circumstances? Was Simeon so ill that they were waiving ordinary hospital rules? Was he... Her eyes closed briefly because she couldn't bear the thought that had slid like a deadly snake into her mind. He couldn't be dying, he mustn't be.

'Are you all right?' asked a young nurse, halting beside her with a searching look, and she started, her eyes opening and a faint flush crawling into her face at the way the girl was staring.

'Yes, I'm fine—I'm looking for Mr Gerard. Sister said he was in the side-ward.'

'Turn left at the end, and you'll see him. He's the only patient in the side-ward at the moment.'

'Thanks,' Juliet said, walking on. Why was Simeon the only patient in this other ward? Because he was dangerously ill and needed absolute quiet?

She turned the corner, a chill finger of fear trailing down her spine, and looked quickly, urgently, at the only bed which was occupied. She was so anxious that her eyes blurred for an instant, and as she paused there, her breathing ragged, the man in the bed turned his head and stared at her.

Then her eyes cleared and she could see him, her blue eyes running over him in a rapid search for clues about his condition. His face was pale, his hair looking very black against his colourless skin, but the only injuries she could see at first did not look serious: a few dark-coloured bruises on one cheek, where the skin was shiny and highly glazed, a cut on his temples just over one eye, a bulky bandage over the palm of one of his hands. Relief made her legs turn rubbery and she leant on the nearest solid object, which happened to be a chair.

'Hello,' she said in a shaky voice, trying to smile, but Simeon did not smile back; in fact he glared at her with what felt like hatred.

'You!' he grated. 'What on earth are you doing here?'

She had been so obsessed with fear that he was seriously ill, or even dying, that it hadn't occurred to her to wonder if he would want to see her. She certainly hadn't expected to be looked at with bitter hostility, and it cut the ground from under her feet.

'I...' she stammered, biting her inner lip. 'I h-heard about the fire on the radio this morning, and...'

'And thought I might be about to join the Choir Immortal, leaving you with everything I owned, I suppose?' he coldly mocked. 'Sorry to disappoint you—I'm not about to die.'

'What a pity!' Juliet snapped, anger sending a flow of adrenalin through her. What on earth made her care so much whether this man lived or died? 'I needn't have come, then!'

'No, you wasted your journey,' he muttered. 'I'm perfectly well.'

'Then why have they kept you in hospital?' She slowly walked over to sit on a chair beside his bed, and noticed something else—that the hair along the right side of his face had an oddly scorched look, as though the flames had leapt past without actually touching.

He grimaced impatiently. 'Oh, they're afraid of shock, mainly—and the after-effects of inhaling smoke. There's nothing seriously wrong with me. In fact, I'm fit enough to leave hospital but they insist on keeping me in for what they laughingly call observation, which entails waking me up every time I drift off to sleep and shining lights in my eyes and banging around my bed shouting questions and offering me food I wouldn't eat if I were going to be hanged in the morning.'

She laced her trembling fingers together in her lap, flushing a little as she realised that he was watching her do so. 'I should think they know what they're doing,' she gently said, and his mouth twisted in derision.

'You must be the perfect patient. You would just do as you're told and not question anything, would you? That isn't the way you behave when I'm around. You never stop arguing with me.'

Her lips parted, a furious retort on her tongue, then she noticed his pallor again, and the dark shadows under his eyes, and she mentally counted to ten before she spoke, changing the subject.

'What about Chantries? Do you know how serious the damage is?'

He leaned back against his piled up pillows with a faint sigh, his expression ironic. 'Nothing irretrievable, thanks to your father.'

'My father?' she repeated, blue eyes wide and dark.

'He was the one who noticed the smoke coming out of my bedroom window and raised the alarm. He was just setting out on his usual prowl around the grounds, in the early hours, looking for poachers, when he spotted the smoke. He raced up to the house, but couldn't raise anyone, so he broke in through the kitchen window, ran up the stairs and apparently found me unconscious on the floor of my bedroom. He dragged me out, then got a fire extinguisher from the wall and went back to put the fire out, but it had too much of a hold, and time was running out, so he shut the door again, and rang the fire brigade and the ambulance service. I knew nothing of all this; I was barely conscious. But I've been told this morning that they managed to contain the fire—because he acted so promptly, it didn't spread any further, and the only damage was to my bedroom. That's pretty extensive, but it could have been a great deal worse.'

Her throat hurt, and she swallowed painfully before she could get out a few husky words. 'A great deal worse,' she agreed. He could have been killed. The thought stabbed like a knife and her eyes glistened with unshed tears so she looked down, hiding that from him.

There was a long silence, then Simeon said coolly, 'Well, as you're here, you might as well be useful. I've had enough of this place and I'm going to sign myself out tomorrow morning, whether the doctors agree or not. I want you to go to Chantries, fetch me some clothes and drive me home tomorrow morning.'

Juliet frowned. 'I don't think you should do that—I'd advise you to——'

'I didn't ask for your advice!' he bit out, and she fell silent.

In any other circumstances, she would have yelled back at him, told him not to give her orders or snarl at her, but she couldn't shout back at a man who looked the way he did. She had never seen him looking ill, or, in fact, even under the weather. She found it deeply disturbing. Until this moment, if anyone had asked her what sort of man Simeon

Gerard was, she wouldn't have hesitated to say, tough, impervious to most human feelings, and even dangerous, if you crossed him. She lowered her lashes and studied him uncertainly through them, tracing the weariness in the way his body lay, slack and still, under the white hospital bedcover, noting the taut white line around his mouth, the way his hands clenched on the sheet. Simeon might not have been burned in the fire, but something disastrous had happened to him—or was this just the effects of shock? But shock could be dangerous, couldn't it? she anxiously reminded herself. Simeon shouldn't leave hospital unless his doctor agreed, she was sure of that.

'Well?' he impatiently grated, lifting his black head from the pillow in an angry movement. 'Will you do as I ask, or won't you?'

She looked up and their eyes met; hers blue, nervous, uncertainly shifting, his a hard, silvery grey. Juliet felt her stomach plunge with painful feeling, a love she could barely conceal, and to distract him from discovering her secret she hurriedly nodded and said, 'Yes, if you insist.'

He gave a little sigh, his head fell back against the pillow and his hands unclenched from the sheet. He closed his eyes, his black lashes lying against the pallor of his cheeks. 'Come around eleven—the specialist will have seen me by then, and I may have permission to go home.'

He didn't add that whatever the specialist said he was going home, but Juliet was left in no doubt about that. She had no time to try again to persuade him against it because just then a nurse walked up to them with a rattling tray, gave her a polite smile and said, 'I'm sorry, but Sister says could you go now? It's lunchtime, and we don't allow visitors at mealtimes.'

Juliet got up. 'Yes, of course——' she began, but before she could move Simeon's hand shot out and grabbed her wrist in an iron lock.

She looked down, her lips parted on a silent intake of air, and his grey eyes glittered up at her. 'Don't forget!'

She nodded, and his hand fell back, leaving her free. She huskily said, 'Well, I'll see you tomorrow, then.' Inside, she ached to kiss him, to smooth the line of pain away from that taut male mouth, but Simeon had closed his eyes again and seemed to have forgotten she existed, so she turned to go, giving the watching nurse a polite smile.

The other girl gave a little chuckle, her eyes dancing with mischief. 'It's OK, you can kiss him, don't mind me!'

Juliet flushed a little and gave Simeon a startled look, finding his grey eyes open again, fixed on her face with a sardonic irony in them that made her stiffen.

It would have been embarrassing to walk away after that; the nurse knew she was Simeon's wife and must have been surprised to see her about to leave without kissing him. Juliet saw she had no option, so she bent quickly to kiss his cheek, but Simeon moved faster. His head shifted on the pillow and her lips touched his mouth instead. He put a hand up to clasp her head and hold it in place while his mouth moved hotly against hers, then he let her go and Juliet shot upright again, her lips trembling and her pulses beating wildly.

She briefly met his eyes, saw the mockery in them, and turned stumbling away. 'Well . . . bye . . .' she muttered.

'See you soon, darling,' Simeon called after her, but she didn't look back. He had been tormenting her deliberately, knowing she couldn't do anything about it. She was angry and humiliated, but helpless, and that amused Simeon even more. She heard him laughing as she turned the corner into the main ward and her teeth met.

She passed the sister as she left the ward and the other woman asked her, 'How did you think your husband looked, Mrs Gerard?'

'Not at all well,' Juliet said. 'He's talking of leaving hospital tomorrow—is that advisable?'

'I wouldn't say it was likely that Mr Stephens, the consultant, who will be seeing him tomorrow, would send him home so soon,' the sister answered warily.

It was impossible, of course, to warn her that Simeon intended to leave, with or without the specialist's permission. Juliet knew he would kill her if she betrayed his conficence, and, anyway, she couldn't conspire against him with the hospital authorities, however much she might disagree with what he was planning.

The ward sister was watching her expression, her smile wry. 'Don't worry, Mrs Gerard, men are always restless and uneasy in hospital.'

Juliet met her eyes, wondering if she knew Simeon's intentions, and the sister calmly said, 'I'm sure Mr Stephens will persuade him to be patient.'

'I hope so,' Juliet said, without much optimism. The other woman did not know Simeon very well if she imagined he was easy to persuade.

Leaving the hospital, she found herself driving in a gentle sunshine through poignantly familiar winding country lanes whose hedges were just coming into leaf. Every turn in the road brought back another memory, and she began to feel unreal. Time slipped backwards in her head. She was a girl, again, suffering the pangs of first love and having no idea how to deal with it.

She would soon reach Chantries. Her stomach plunged with sick reaction to the idea. She had never thought she would see it again. It was crazy to think of going there. He must have someone looking after the house, who could take him his clothes, drive him home. It didn't have to be her.

Yet she kept on driving, as though unable to turn back to London, and safety. Here and there beneath the hedges she glimpsed buttery pale primroses among the grass, spring was well under way in this milder weather, she thought, her eyes following a blackbird taking off from a field with nesting material in his beak: straw and twigs and moss. He had gathered too much, his flight was unsteady and she kept expecting him to crash land, but he vanished into some trees.

She wished it wasn't spring; it made her feel restless, frustrated. But it was more than that, she admitted to herself. Spring was a lovely time of year; the air was warmer, the light more brilliant. It was a time to be happy, not to ache with pain as she did.

Simeon bewildered her, baffled her. Why, if he seriously wanted her to go back to him and give him a child, hadn't he followed her to London when she'd fled from the cottage? Why hadn't he been in touch with her since, either?

He had come down to the cottage in a mood of overbearing determination, so set on getting his own way that she had almost given in—what had happened to change his mind? She couldn't believe that he had found Adam a threat. She had seen no sign of it. In face-to-face confrontation Simeon had been very sure of himself, coolly derisive. It had been Adam who had lost control of his temper without making any impact on Simeon, not the other way around.

She bit her lip, angry with herself for her own contradictory feelings. She had run away, had told herself she wanted to get away, yet all the time she had expected him to follow her; she had been on edge day and night because he hadn't. She ought to make up her mind what she did want, not vacillate back and forth.

She was still arguing with herself when she crested a hill and got her first sight of Chantries, the spring sunshine lingering on warm red brick, great decorated chimneys, uneven, faded tiles, rows of high sash windows. Even from this distance the house pulled at you, beckoning like an alluring hand. It was not one of those houses built to be a stately home, to impress and overawe. Chantries had been intended to be a family home, welcoming its master back from hunting on winter evenings, or from work on the farm, or guests coming to dine or stay. The chimneys told of huge fireplaces in which logs would burn with a crackle, of shadowy, comfortable rooms with shutters at the windows and lamps glowing when night fell.

The house lay within a small park: a sea of green turf on which she could see sheep grazing. A few oaks and elms were scattered around the park, in summer making dark pools of shadow where the sheep lay when the sun was high. Beyond the park stretched the woods, which her father patrolled, but Juliet's eyes were drawn towards the little orchard she could just glimpse at the back of the house, and beyond that to the cottage where she had been born and grown up, and which was still her father's home.

She had never forgiven her father for what happened that night, in the orchard, for the expression on his face, the cruel things he had said to her. The last thing she wanted was to see him.

If he knew that she had arrived, out of the blue, at Chantries, what would he do? Ignore the news? Carefully avoid her? Or would he come to the house to see her?

Her pale mouth moved in a cynical curve. No, not that. Her father was a man who didn't forgive or forget. He wouldn't want to see her again. If she kept out of his way, he would keep out of hers, she could be sure of that.

She drove through the open decorated iron park gates, with their elaborate scroll-work set around inked initials, a finely wrought 'G' for Gerard and 'R' for Robert, the initials of the eighteenth-century Gerard who had had the gates made. From there the drive wound up to the house, flat turf on either side. Juliet drove slowly, staring at the upper floor and seeing for the first time visible evidence of the fire: charred and blackened window-frames, the smoke-darkened red brick around them. A tarpaulin had been erected inside the glass-less window, to keep out the weather, so that it was impossible to glimpse the interior of the room and see what damage had been done internally.

She parked on the gravel in front of the house, got out and looked uncertainly at the great oak front door. It was the original one: massive, studded with iron, with tongues of thick iron running across it from each hinge. Bolted inside, it would withstand a battering-ram.

She stared at it, at the blind windows, and felt panic flood through her. She couldn't go through with it. She couldn't go into that house. She had to get away.

She was about to get back into her car when she heard footsteps grate on the gravel and swung around just as her father came round the corner of the house.

Juliet went white with shock, and Jack Newcome stopped dead, his head lowered and his body as tense as that of a bull about to charge. They stared at each other without moving or speaking for what seemed an eternity.

Her eyes were dazedly taking in impressions, though, realising all sorts of things that startled and confused her. He had aged more than she had expected, for a start. His hair was quite white, his shoulders had a heavy stoop, he had lost a lot of weight, almost shrunk. He's an old man! she thought, with a stab of shock.

Jack Newcome was staring at her, too, his grizzled brows drawn in a frown that was incredulous.

'Juliet?' His voice was low and rough, as if he didn't quite believe his eyes. 'Is that you?'

'Yes,' she said huskily. 'How are you, Father?' The name came out instinctively, but with a blurred sound.

Her father moved closer, slowly, still staring. 'You . . . you're so different . . .'

'I'm eight years older.' It was only to be expected that she would have changed a great deal—after all, she had been a teenager when she'd run away. Now she was a full-grown woman. But she hadn't expected her father to change so much. He had seemed to her to stay the same all through her childhood and adolescence—he had hardly altered, except inwardly, even when her mother had left. Jack Newcome had become bitter, had hardened, turned in on himself, after that. But physically he had stayed the same: a man toughened by years of outdoor life, muscled, wiry, very fit. Now, though, he was no longer the man he had once been.

He came to a standstill, right in front of her, and she realised that they were almost the same height, which startled, if not shocked her. He had once seemed to tower over her. Now she could look straight into his eyes.

'What are you doing here, Juliet?'

'I heard the news on the radio... about the fire, Simeon——' she began in a confused voice and her father's face darkened, his mouth twisting.

'Oh, I see! And you came to find out if you were a wealthy widow, I suppose! Well, you can stop hoping, because——'

'Stop it, Father!' she angrily interrupted. 'I came because I was so scared when I heard, I was afraid Sim might die, and I...'

She couldn't put into words, even to herself, but the truth of how she felt came out, clear and simple. Jack Newcome listened to it, his brows drawn, his face grim.

'If you care for him, why did you go away?'

'That's our business, not yours!' She was still angry, her head thrown back defiantly, and her blue eyes telling him without words that she was an adult now, not a child, and he had no right to bully or even question her.

'It was me who was left here after you'd gone, to face everyone!' he accused, scowling. 'Folk talked of nothing else for months. Everyone I met stared at me—oh, they pretended to be sorry for me, sweet as sugar to my face, but I knew they were all grinning and whispering behind my back. Nothing better to do, most of them. Kids, too, peering over hedges, or round trees at me, calling things, then runnng off!' He broke off, swallowing convulsively. 'First my wife runs off, then my child... Can you wonder they all thought it was my fault, I was to blame?'

She had hated him for years, had blamed him, thought it was all his fault, but a strange mixture of pity and regret made her say gently, 'No, it wasn't your fault, Father. I ran away from Simeon, not you. He knows why I ran away—it had nothing to do with you.'

Jack Newcome fixed his eyes bleakly on her face. 'Then why haven't you been in touch with me since?'

'I'm sorry—I was unhappy, I just wanted to forget...' She made a sweeping gesture that took in the house, the grounds, him. 'Everything! I closed the door because I couldn't bear to remember.' She gazed into his eyes, a look of pleading on her face. 'You can understand that, can't you, Father?' His marriage had been a disaster, and he had had to survive its break-up somehow. He hadn't gone away physically, but she remembered how he had been during the years when she was growing up, and she knew that he had gone away in spirit, closed the door on everyone around him, including her.

Jack Newcome stood very still, his eyes blank as they stared at her, and for a moment she thought he would reject her appeal for sympathy, then a deep sigh shook him and he nodded. 'Yes, I can understand...'

It was the first time they had ever talked as adults, made any sort of real connection, and the surprise of it made them look away, falling silent. Juliet bit her lip and looked through her lowered lashes at him, not sure what to say now. The one thing about him that was familiar was his clothes; he still wore his rough, shabby old tweed jacket, a faded khaki shirt, which as a child she had imagined he wore because it reminded him of his time in the army, his worn corduroy trousers, the wide leather belt around the waist. Now, though, they all hung on him; the body inside them had withered, and she felt a prick of tears behind her eyes. She didn't know this man, had never known him, and soon it would be too late.

Huskily, she said, 'I've been to the hospital. I saw Simeon, he sent me here...he told me you saved his life...'

'Nothing of the kind!' her father gruffly interrupted. 'I just happened to notice the fire before it got a hold. Some local reporter was here an hour or two back, trying to build it up into something heroic, but all I did was wake Sim up.'

'He thinks he wouldn't have woken up,' she said, smiling at him. 'He thinks he would be dead now if it wasn't for you.'

'Nonsense!' Jack Newcome had gone a little red and was scowling again. He was a brave man who hated to have his courage talked about. He had never been one for talking much. He spent his days mostly alone, out in the open, with animals and birds for company, and had little contact with his own kind, which was how he apparently liked it, but Juliet watched him, wondering if that was now as true as it had once been. There were lines of loneliness in his face, a bleakness in his eyes. He was an old man now and he was always alone.

Shrugging, he changed the subject. 'Are you going to stay at Chantries while you're here?'

'He asked me to come and collect his clothes,' she said and her father exclaimed in surprise.

'They're never sending him home so soon! He was in a bad way when I dragged him out of that room.'

She hid a smile at that admission of his courage in saving Simeon from the fire.

'I doubt if the hospital will approve, but he's determined to come home, whether they like it or not.'

'The fool!' muttered Jack Newcome and Juliet laughed shortly.

'You know Simeon.'

'Oh, I know him—stubborn as a mule and twice as stupid! Can't you talk him out of it?'

'I tried, but he just yelled at me to do as I was told and bring him his clothes. I suppose they weren't all burnt in the fire?'

Her father shook his head. 'Not so far as I know! All the furniture that wasn't ruined has been moved into the next room—only the stuff on the side of the room where the fire started was badly damaged.'

'What caused the fire?'

'The electric wiring—it's as old as the hills, it all needs replacing.' He looked at her uncertainly. 'Are you nervous of staying overnight in case another fire breaks out? Maybe you had better sleep on the ground floor—the housekeeper had a little suite of rooms next to the kitchen, and the wiring in that was done when the suite was modernised. You'll have to make up a bed for yourself, I'm afraid.'

'No need, I'll probably go to a hotel,' she said, nervous of even entering the house, and he frowned.

'Why pay good money when you can stay here for free? After all, you're Sim's wife—you've the right, I'm sure he must have meant you to...'

'Maybe he did, but I don't think I can face a lot of stares and questions! I suppose he has a housekeeper?'

'There was one, but after his father died Simeon told her he didn't need her any more, as there was just him in the house. Now, he has a woman from the village come in on weekdays, to clean and cook for him, but she went an hour ago, when she'd done all she could in his bedroom—so there's nobody here to ask questions or be curious, don't worry.' He turned towards the front door, producing a bundle of keys from his pocket. 'I have the key, I can let you in.'

Juliet felt very odd as she stepped over that threshold again, for the first time in eight years. The whole weight of the past seemed to descend upon her shoulders.

She almost cried out against all those bitter memories, and then the sun shone past her into the old, shadowy, panelled hall, revealing the beauty she had forgotten. The sunken red-flagged floors shining with years of loving polish, the high beamed roof, the great stone fireplace in which stood a tall vase of spring flowers, their scent sweet on the air, and she realised that somehow she was free of the guilt and resentment and misery she had been carrying around for so long.

# CHAPTER NINE

'IF YOU'RE determined to be foolish, I can't stop you,' the ward sister said coldly. 'But I must warn you——'

'I've had all the warnings! Skip the repeat dose and show me where to sign.' Simeon's tone was firm enough to silence the woman, whose lips set thinly before she pushed a form at him, silently indicating where he should put his signature.

Juliet stood beside him, flushed, very conscious of the sister's irritated, reproachful gaze. Nobody had noticed the case she'd carried into the ward; Simeon had taken the clothes and vanished into a bathroom to re-emerge fully clothed in grey trousers and a thick blue roll-necked sweater which gave his grey eyes a warmer colour. He was still pale, the burns on his cheek angry-looking, but dressed he seemed much more himself, almost normal.

'My father chose those for you,' she had told him. 'He could have brought them here, too. You didn't need me.'

'I'll decide what I need,' he had said casually, and her colour had risen. She fought with her stupid feelings, terrified of him seeing and understanding them, but she needn't have bothered. He wasn't there to observe her. He was already going, walking away through the ward and startling the young nurse who was giving out pills to some other patient. Her mouth had dropped open, and she had squeaked after him, 'Oh! Mr Gerard... what... where...?'

Juliet had scuttled after his long-legged, striding figure and tried not to think about what he had just said. He might 'need' her to have his child, but that was a purely material necessity; it wasn't the sort of need she felt for him.

Sister had barred their way, astonished and furious at seeing him fully dressed, and had begun a long argument with him that Simeon had just ended in a peremptory tone. She had tried to draw Juliet into the discussion, but Simeon had said curtly, 'Leave my wife out of this! She just did what I told her.'

Juliet had been glad to stay out of the squabble, but she had been on the ward sister's side, although she'd said nothing. Simeon had no business leaving hospital so early; he couldn't possibly be fit enough. She knew him too well to try to argue with him, however, so she tried to look quietly submissive, no ally for the sister's defeated army, and got a scornful glance from the other woman for her pains.

The necessary form signed, they walked out of the hospital to where Juliet had parked her car. Simeon made for the driver's seat but Juliet slipped past him at the last moment, her hand seizing the door-handle, her chin up in defiance.

'I'll drive, thanks. It *is* my car.'

He considered her expression, his eyes speculative. 'If you insist!' he said at last.

'I do.' She unlocked the door, pushed the empty suitcase into the back and got behind the wheel, slightly unsteady after that little confrontation, but triumphant, too, because she had won, he had backed down. It had been a very minor victory, but it was a victory, all the same.

Simeon slid into the seat next to her, stretching his long legs with a sigh. 'You don't know how glad I am to get out of that place!'

'I expect they're glad to see you go, even though they felt duty-bound to try to stop you,' Juliet said, starting the engine. 'You aren't exactly the ideal patient.'

He was watching her, his head turned sideways against the back of the seat, and she found his stare unnerving, wondering what he was thinking. 'What happened with your father?' he asked quietly at last.

'We talked.' There was no way she could explain to anyone what had happened when she met her father again; it had been unexpected and disturbing to realise that they were in a sense meeting for the first time, two total strangers. Eight years had made such radical changes in them both; she had come to maturity and her father had grown old. Time had burnt away their differences, resolved all their anger. They had come to terms with themselves, and the past, and with all that out of the way they had been free to get to know each other at last.

'Well, well,' Simeon drawled. 'Who would have thought it?'

'Thought what?' She knew what that amazed tone meant, but she kept her eyes on the road, watching a little white sports car which had come up behind her out of nowhere and was trying to pass her in spite of the zigzag bend just ahead which made the manoeuvre both dangerous and stupid.

'I'm not quite sure, actually,' Simeon murmured thoughtfully. 'Does it mean that you've really grown up—or that your father has finally seen some sense?'

'Both, maybe,' she conceded, a half-smile curving her mouth.

'And how does it feel?' he enquired, and she considered her reply a moment.

'Disconcerting.'

He laughed. 'I'm sure.'

The white car shot past with a roar of tyres and a snarl of acceleration, and narrowly missed being flattened by a juggernaut bearing down on it from the other direction. The juggernaut blared angrily, the sports car hooted back, and then both disappeared, leaving the road to Juliet's car.

She whistled under her breath. 'I really thought he'd had it, the crazy idiot.'

'It was a woman,' Simeon said.

'You weren't even looking at the car! That's pure male chauvinism.'

'No, it's observation,' he said, his smile infuriating. 'I recognised the car. She lives near Chantries. Andrea Jameson; she works as a freelance designer and goes up to London quite often.' He slipped Juliet a sidelong glance. 'A very sexy little blonde, too. I'd bet on it that every male for twenty miles has noticed her.'

'Well, if she always drives like that she won't live long,' Juliet snapped, angrily aware of a jealous ache behind her ribs. How many women had there been in his life since she'd left? Eight years was a long time. He wasn't the celibate type, either. He had too fierce a sex drive. Were any of the women still around, was he seeing anyone? In many ways, he was a stranger to her—she knew almost nothing about him or his private life, although he had been her husband now for eight years.

'Which bedroom did you use at Chantries?' he asked, breaking into her thoughts, and she jumped so violently that she lost control of the steering-wheel. The car swerved across the carriageway, and a car coming towards them angrily sounded its horn.

Juliet dragged on the wheel, righting the car, and drove on, very flushed and furious with herself.

She darted a look at Simeon, who was heavy browed, and snapped, 'Don't say a single, solitary word!'

'OK, just stop the car,' he said grimly.

'Don't be ridiculous. What are you going to do, hitch a lift?'

'I'm driving the rest of the way, Juliet. I want to get there in one piece.'

'You can forget that!' she said, putting her foot down, half afraid he would grab the wheel. The car leapt forward and Simeon's frown deepened, but he couldn't risk a fight over control of the car while they were doing that speed, so he had to sit there, glowering at her, his long, lean body poised and menacing whenever she glimpsed it out of the corner of her eye.

Ten minutes later they pulled up outside Chantries and Simeon slid out of the passenger seat, came round and opened the driver's door and caught hold of her arm with iron fingers.

'Get out of there!'

She got out but dragged herself free of his grip. 'Don't manhandle me!'

'You risked both our lives!' he accused, and she knew it was true, but she certainly wasn't admitting it to him. The hostility she felt burnt like a fire in peat; deep and slow and unreachable. Her blue eyes smouldered with it and Simeon stared down into them, his face taut.

'You shouldn't have made me jump like that, shouting at me!' she muttered and his mouth twisted.

'I didn't shout. I spoke quite quietly, in fact. That wasn't what made you so jumpy, and you know it. We both know it. Just being alone with me in a car makes you as nervous as hell—do you want me to tell you why?'

'I know why! Because I hate the sight of you!' She got the keys to the house, which her father had given her the previous evening, out of her purse, and offered them to Simeon. 'Here, you let yourself into the house. I'm going.'

'Still running away, Juliet?' His grey eyes glittered scornfully and she bit into her inner lip, forcing herself to calm down, to sound perfectly confident. She must not let him see any sign of weakness, of uncertainty; he would seize it and use it to his own advantage.

'I have to get back to London—I want to see my mother and stepfather when they arrive there,' she said in a quietly rational voice. 'They flew home last night, but I haven't been able to get in touch with them yet, and we have a lot to discuss.'

'So do we!'

She shook her head, somehow managing a little smile. 'We've said all we had to say, Simeon. I don't want to...' She broke off, a jab of alarm hitting her, as he closed his eyes and swayed back against the car, his skin very pale. 'Sim!' she said, her arm going round him to support him. 'What is it? Do you feel faint?'

He leaned on her, the weight of his lean, muscled body quite surprising, and murmured incoherently. 'Mmm...'

She looked around in desperation, in the hope of spotting her father, or the woman from the village who worked in the house and who had arrived that morning just as she was leaving, but there was no sign of anyone around.

'Can you walk to the house, if I help you?' she asked him, wondering if she should get him back into the car and drive him back to the hospital.

He seemed to force his eyes open, his body still heavy against her. 'What? Oh, yes, I think so.'

'Maybe I ought to drive back to the hospital!' she thought aloud, not knowing quite what to do.

'No, I'll be fine soon, I'm better already,' he said, and he was beginning to look better, it was true, so she slowly guided him towards the house, took the keys he limply held, and unlocked the front door. Simeon managed to stagger, with her help, into the sitting-room and collapse on to a couch. He still had an arm around her, and somehow he managed to pull her down, too. She was startled by that, a little gasp escaping her, and was too late to stop herself tumbling down beside him. He took her unawares; for a moment she didn't understand, her blue eyes wide and confused as she stared up at him.

It was she who was lying on the couch—it should be Simeon, but he was leaning over her, and she couldn't fathom how that had happened. Only as his hands pressed her down among the cushions on the couch did it begin to dawn on her.

She searched his face, suspicion now a certainty. The weak, helpless look had completely vanished. This was the face she knew only too well, the hard, determined face of the man who had wrecked her life once before already and was apparently intent on doing it again.

'You aren't feeling faint at all!' she accused him, flushing to her hairline.

Simeon watched her back with a mockery that made her feel like screaming.

What a fool she had been! Hadn't she learnt by now never to trust him an inch? He wasn't ill. He hadn't been feeling faint; it had all been acting. It had all been a trick to get her into the house, on to this couch, all alone here with him, and it had worked perfectly.

'I wasn't standing outside my own house arguing the point with you,' Simeon said, quite unashamed of his cheating.

'You lied to me!'

'I didn't tell you anything! I shut my eyes and leaned on you and you jumped to conclusions.'

'You meant me to!'

'I had to talk to you. You were going to run away again, and I couldn't let you.'

'I am not making some cold-blooded bargain with you just so that you can keep Chantries and I can make some money. I don't need money that much. I don't need it at all.'

'And I don't need Chantries,' he said in a deep, harsh voice, making her eyes widen in shock and disbelief.

'What do you take me for?' she burst out, trembling with rage, white with it. 'What sort of fool do you think I am, if you imagine I'm going to believe that for one instant!'

'I'm more of a fool than you are,' he said, his smile bitter with a self-derision that made her wince. 'If I wasn't I would have come after you when you drove off with your London boyfriend. I'd have crashed into your flat, beaten the living daylights out of him, and dragged you off down here by the hair and made you give me what I wanted!'

'Nothing would have made me!' she furiously insisted.

His eyes were wry. 'Be honest with yourself. You know I could have got you into bed, and I wouldn't have had to use force.'

She went crimson, her lips parted to shout a denial at him but no words came out; she was unable to lie but not prepared to make any dangerous admissions.

She didn't need to; he read her expression and smiled crookedly. 'Yes. You and I have always felt that attraction, haven't we? Our minds may not always understand each other, but our bodies seem to. But I didn't follow you, because I was paralysed—just as I was when you ran out on me the first time.'

She seemed to stop breathing, she couldn't swallow, her mouth dry and her ears deafened. What did he mean? Was this another lie, another scheme to make her weaken, give in to him?

'The morning after our wedding, when I woke up and found you gone, it was like being pole-axed,' he said slowly, grimacing. 'At first, I was going to go after you. I wanted to get you back, and I felt like a swine after the way I'd treated you the night before. I knew why you had run. Of course I did. And I felt as guilty as hell——'

'You were!' she muttered, and he didn't argue, just frowned, nodding.

'Yes—I was old enough to know better, I have to take all the blame. But it was more complicated than that. I sat in my car arguing with myself for hours, in a country lane a few miles away, trying to make up my mind what to do, but there was something holding me back, stopping me from moving. It wasn't just the guilt, or the anger, it was worry over you. You were so young, too young to realise what marriage meant.'

'I knew what it meant! I was young, yes, but not that young!' she said huskily. 'That wasn't what made me run away. You've admitted it yourself—you drove me away, you were never in love with me! You hated me. You wanted to hurt me, you were furious with me because you felt you had been forced to marry me.'

'I was angry because we had been forced into a shotgun marriage,' Simeon said roughly. 'I didn't think you were old enough, or in any way ready, for a real marriage.'

'You didn't want to marry me at all!' she cried out, the deeply embedded hurt of it in her blue eyes.

'I hadn't thought of marriage,' he admitted in a heavy, reluctant voice. 'That's true. For heaven's sake, you were a schoolgirl! I was feeling guilty enough because I knew I wanted you like hell and you were just a kid. I kept telling myself to keep my hands off you, but you had other ideas, and I lost my head every time you came close to me. Have you any idea how much that made me despise myself? I tried to stay away from you, but I couldn't, you were the sexiest thing I've ever seen. Sweet seventeen and dying to be kissed, and I was dying to be the one to do the kissing. Only I was no teenager, and a few kisses weren't enough for me. Once I started touching you, I wanted more. I wanted everything. And it made it worse that I soon realised you wanted it, too. You were damnably erotic, Juliet; sensual and sweet and generous—and you drove me wild.'

She had begun to shake, her whole body aching with desire and a wild, uncertain hope. If he meant it...if he loved her... But he hadn't mentioned love, had he? He had talked about wanting her, about passion, never love.

'Then it all exploded around me,' he grimly said. 'And I had to make a choice there and then—what else could I do but say I'd marry you? I hadn't had the time to be certain that was what I wanted, but it had crossed my mind now and then that one day...maybe...when you were older, and knew for sure you wanted me, we might get married. On the other hand, you might fall out of love with me in a month or two. I guessed you were just infatuated with me.'

He looked down into her blue eyes and Juliet hid their expression by letting her lashes droop. She wasn't sure how she had felt eight years ago; whether the explosive mix inside her had been pure chemical reaction, teenage infatuation, or real love. She knew what she felt now—her love for him was tearing her apart—but she wasn't going to let Simeon guess that.

'That was all it was, wasn't it, Juliet?' he asked in a quiet voice and she answered, still without meeting his eyes.

'I suppose so...' Then she looked up at him. 'We should just have been to bed together and made sure we didn't get caught.'

His mouth twisted. 'That was just the trouble— I couldn't do that, either, not to you. You meant too much, and that's why I lost control on our wedding night. No excuse, I know. I regretted it bitterly next day, but I was full of rage because I felt trapped and yet I still wanted you, even though I blamed you and your father. I didn't mean to hurt you, I meant to be gentle, to make that first time easy for you, but once I started making love to you it all got out of hand.'

'You frightened me!' she broke out. 'I hadn't expected it to hurt, nobody had told me...what it would be like...' She had had no mother to talk to, and what she had learnt in school had been a mix of boring sex lessons with drawings she couldn't quite follow and found ugly, and the half-baked versions whispered by friends. Her confused emotions about Simeon hadn't seemed to have any connection with all that.

'I know,' he gently said, frowning. 'Do you think I hadn't realised that? You were so young, I should never have...' He broke off, sighing. 'But I lost my head. I wanted you too much, Juliet, I couldn't keep myself on a lead once I'd started to touch you, but when I woke up and found you gone I knew what I'd done and I felt sick. That was why I didn't follow you and make you come back. If I had, we might both have been hurt a damn sight more. I had to let you go then, to find yourself, to grow

SHOTGUN WEDDING          181

up—and so I went home and my father rang your
mother to find out if you were there. Once we knew
you were safe, I settled down to wait. I thought
that if you had any real feeling for me you would
be back. At first, I thought it would just be months,
at most a year or so—and then as time passed I
had to admit you were never coming back and I
almost hated you.'

'I could see that, when you turned up down in
Cornwall,' she said with a wry grimace. 'And there
was no almost about it. You hated me, especially
after your father died and you read his will.' She
looked into his grey eyes, searching them for the
truth. 'And that's what this is all about now, isn't
it? Chantries. You said a few mintues ago that you
didn't need Chantries, but that isn't true. You love
the place, you always have, and you'd do anything
to get it.'

'No,' he said curtly.

'Oh, I think so!' Her face was bitter with
accusation and distrust.

'When I said I didn't need Chantries, I meant
every word!' Simeon bit out. 'I may have talked
cold-bloodedly, down in Cornwall, but do you
really believe I'd have forced you to sleep with me,
have my baby, if I thought you hated the idea? After
I read the will I was blazingly angry, it's true. I
thought about it, and it occurred to me that,
whatever else you might have got up to since I last
saw you, you hadn't got married again. You were
still my wife. That was when the idea hit me. I
couldn't lose anything by seeing you, telling you

the terms of the will. You might even come back
to me. Eight years was a long time—I thought it
was worth trying, and...' His mouth twisted. 'And
I wanted to see you again. As soon as I'd started
thinking about it, I liked it more and more, especially after I'd tracked you down in Cornwall and
realised you were ten times sexier and lovelier than
you had ever been. And I thought you were
attracted to me, too.'

He was watching her closely, eyes narrowed, but
Juliet evaded his gaze, looking down, her lashes
brushing her flushed cheek.

He sighed, and said, 'Well, then the other guy
turned up, and you ran out on me again, for the
second time, and knocked me for six. I thought it
meant I'd got it completely wrong; you didn't give
a damn for me. It looked as if you preferred the
other guy, after all. I found it hard to believe, but
then women are baffling creatures—they seem to
pick the oddest men. I wasn't running after you,
just to get slapped in the face again—my pride
wouldn't let me. I went back to Chantries to lick
my wounds and got in touch with my solicitor, told
him I wanted him to start divorce proceedings at
once.'

She stared up at him, hardly breathing.

'You did?'

He took the quesiton for disbelief, and snarled
at her. 'Yes, I did!'

'OK, OK,' she said mildly. 'No need to shout!'

'Then stop querying everything I say!' His grey
eyes glittered into hers, his face as hard as planed

wood. 'Lawyers take their time, but your solicitor should hear from mine in a month or so.'

Her mouth was dry. If it was true, why had he done it?

Simeon's mouth indented. 'My solicitor thought I was mad, of course, knowing the terms of my father's will, and tried to talk me out of it, but I told him to mind his own business and get on with the job. By now he has probably begun the long drawn out process. It takes ages for a divorce to come through, you know.'

'Well, after eight years, who's in a hurry?' Juliet huskily said, and his eyes flashed in rage.

'Don't make jokes about it, damn you! I don't find any of this funny. I came back to Chantries feeling like death. Why do you think I didn't wake up when my room caught fire? I rarely drink these days—what happened on our wedding night cured me of drinking much—but the other night I was going out of my mind. I couldn't sleep, couldn't think about anything but you, and I had to shut down somehow. I hit the whisky for a few hours, fell into bed and slept like the dead. That was why your father had to drag me out of the room.'

She had paled, biting her lip. 'Sim, I'm sorry——'

'Don't say that!' he said hoarsely, and then he swooped down on her, his lips clamping over hers, stifling the little cry she gave. Her mouth parted under the heated possession of that kiss—she couldn't fight him, or the sensual fire which he was lighting deep inside her body. Her arms went round his neck and she yielded, kissing him back hungrily, her fingers in his hair. His hand moved between them, slipped inside her shirt to find her warm flesh, softly caressed her breasts, making her shudder with desire.

It had been so hard to stop him, to run away from what she wanted desperately, but this time she knew she wouldn't stop him; this time, at last, she was going to let it happen. She loved him, she had loved him for years, ever since she had been a very young girl and not quite ready for love. Simeon was right; she had been too young. The overwhelming force of her own emotions had drowned her and she had been right to flee. He had been wise not to come after her, too. Love had come too soon. It had not been the right time for them. Now was their time, and she clung to him, her mouth igniting his desire while she moved against him wildly, restlessly, passion taking over her whole body.

When Simeon broke off that kiss, it almost sent her into shock, her blue eyes opening wide, startled, her bruised mouth parted in a cry of protest. She still clung to him, her hands dragging at his hair, trying to pull him down to her again, but he shook his head, his mouth wry with regret.

'No, darling. Not yet. We aren't being stampeded into it this time, not even by ourselves. We're going to start again, and do it properly—we'll get married again.'

'What?' She was half dazed with passion, and couldn't understand what he was saying. His grey eyes gleamed in sudden, warm amusement and he dropped a light kiss on her eyes.

'Wake up, darling! Don't you see? If we sleep together now, this minute, you'll start suspecting me again—you won't believe I want you, you'll think it was all for Chantries. But it isn't, Juliet.' His voice deepened, dark with a feeling which made her go weak. 'I love you. I don't know quite what I felt eight years ago: a pretty unstable mix of sexual attraction and affection, I think; but I do know it didn't die because you went away. It just smouldered on, right down inside me, and when I saw you again it burst into flames.'

She ran her fingers through his hair, smiling into his eyes, her lips trembling a little. 'Oh, Sim...I know...I felt exactly the same. I'd thought it was all over, and then there you were, and I was lost.'

He kissed her fiercely, held her close, murmuring husky words of passion. 'I want you so much, Juliet. You don't know——'

'I do,' she said, her voice shaky with laughter and desire. 'Oh, yes, I do...' She stroked his flushed face, feeling the heat in his skin and excited by that evidence of how he felt. 'Sim, when I think that it so nearly went wrong—you might have divorced me, we might never have met again, if your room hadn't caught fire!'

He laughed softly. 'Thank God it did! If there had been no fire, you wouldn't have come back here, and I would never have discovered that you did care!'

She gave a little shiver, frowning. 'Frightening, isn't it?' Every time she thought about it she felt she was staring into a black abyss.

'I'm trying not to look too closely,' admitted Simeon, his expression grim. 'Such a narrow margin—between losing you, and being happy! But there was a fire, and you came. Maybe if you hadn't heard about the fire, fate would have come up with something else. Who knows? We have a second chance, that's all that matters—let's take it and this time make it work, Juliet. That's why I want to go through a second ceremony—this time we'll do it in church, have our marriage blessed. And we'll take a honeymoon somewhere romantic and start married life the right way.'

She loved the idea; she smiled, already working out what she would wear for the church blessing— not white, but a soft cream lace and silk dress she could wear again for parties. Her mind was busy, imagining it. She would insist that her mother and Giorgio came. Her father would have to meet his ex-wife again some time—once she and Simeon were living together, he couldn't ignore her mother when she visited, and once there were children Juliet knew she would need her mother around as often as possible.

A little frown caught her brows together. 'Sim...what am I going to do about my job?'

'We'll have to work something out, won't we?' he said without urgency, and she looked up at him and relaxed again, smiling.

There were going to be problems; they would work them out somehow, together. There would be a solution, and they would find it—she had no doubts about that, any more than she had doubts about Simeon's love for her. He had hit the nail right on the head when he'd said they were fated—it had always been meant that they should come together, and now that at last they had they would be able to make it work.

## BARBARY WHARF

**An exciting six-book series, one title per month
beginning in October, by bestselling author**

Set in the glamorous and fast-paced world of international
journalism, BARBARY WHARF will take you from the
*Sentinel*'s hectic newsroom to the most thrilling cities in the
world. You'll meet media tycoon Nick Caspian and his
adversary Gina Tyrrell, whose dramatic story of passion and
heartache develops throughout the six-book series.

In book one, BESIEGED (#1498), you'll also meet Hazel and
Piet. Hazel's always had a good word to say about everyone.
Well, almost. She just can't stand Piet Van Leyden, Nick's
chief architect and one of the most arrogant know-it-alls she's
ever met! As far as Hazel's concerned, Piet's a twentieth-
century warrior, and she's the one being besieged!

Don't miss the sparks in the first BARBARY WHARF
book, BESIEGED (#1498), available in October from
Harlequin Presents.

# JAYNE ANN KRENTZ

A two-part epic tale from one of today's most popular romance novelists!

---

## Dreams
### Parts One & Two

*The warrior died at her feet, his blood running out of the cave entrance and mingling with the waterfall. With his last breath he cursed the woman— told her that her spirit would remain chained in the cave forever until a child was created and born there....*

So goes the ancient legend of the Chained Lady and the curse that bound her throughout the ages—until destiny brought Diana Prentice and Colby Savager together under the influence of forces beyond their understanding. Suddenly they were both haunted by dreams that linked past and present, while their waking hours were filled with danger. Only when Colby, Diana's modern-day warrior, learned to love, could those dark forces be vanquished. Only then could Diana set the Chained Lady free....

---

 **Available in September wherever Harlequin books are sold.**

JK92

# WELCOME TO

**The quintessential small town, where everyone knows everybody else!**

Finally, books that capture the pleasure of tuning in to your favorite TV show!

**GREAT READING...GREAT SAVINGS...AND A FABULOUS FREE GIFT!**

Each book set in Tyler is a self-contained love story; together, the twelve novels stitch the fabric of the community. The covers honor the old American tradition of quilting; each cover depicts a patch of the large Tyler quilt.

With Tyler you can receive a fabulous gift, ABSOLUTELY FREE, by collecting proofs-of-purchase found in each Tyler book. And use our special Tyler coupons to save on your next TYLER book purchase.

Join your friends at Tyler for the seventh book, ARROWPOINT by Suzanne Ellison, available in September.

*Rumors fly about the death at the old lodge! What happens when Renata Meyer finds an ancient Indian sitting cross-legged on her lawn?*

**Back by Popular Demand**

# Janet Dailey
## Americana

Janet Dailey takes you on a romantic tour of America through fifty favorite Harlequin Presents novels, each one set in a different state and researched by Janet and her husband, Bill.

A journey of a lifetime. The perfect collectible series!

September titles
### #39 RHODE ISLAND
*Strange Bedfellow*
### #40 SOUTH CAROLINA
*Low Country Liar*